## "So, we've got dilemmas in contraception before lunch, and what about after lunch?"

"Antenatal care, then tea, and then the role of HRT in menopause and premature ovarian failure."

Katharine's cup rattled in her saucer and she put it down abruptly. "Lots of material there, then," she said lightly, and wondered why she'd chosen to come on this course instead of all the many others she could have selected as part of her ongoing vocational training. Now she didn't know how she was going to get through that particular seminar with Oliver at her side, without him realizing something was wrong.

And that, of course, was something she had to avoid at all costs. If he ever got wind of why she'd left him then, being the man he was, he'd be so busy doing the decent thing that he wouldn't do what was right for him. And then he'd never have the children he longed for.

Dear Reader,

Never go back. That's what we're always told, but there are times when you need to in order to get closure. And there are times when, despite the fact that you don't want to go back, you have no choice, because the past comes to find you. So it was for Kate and Oliver. Their past was cluttered with misunderstanding and deception, but underlying it all was a deep and abiding love. Without that chance meeting...

And it was another chance meeting that led to me finding out about Prader-Willi Syndrome. I'd never heard of it, but some friends shared their story with me, and I would like to thank them for allowing me to use elements of it, and for the warmth and generosity of their friendship.

Researching case histories adds a fascinating and often heartrending dimension to my job as a storyteller. I hope it does the same for you as a reader.

Enjoy this book, with my love, and have a wonderful Christmas.

Caroline

# For Christmas, For Always

## Caroline Anderson

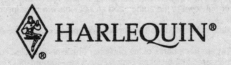

TORONTO • NEW YORK • LONDON
AMSTERDAM • PARIS • SYDNEY • HAMBURG
STOCKHOLM • ATHENS • TOKYO • MILAN • MADRID
PRAGUE • WARSAW • BUDAPEST • AUCKLAND

ISBN 0-373-06435-7

FOR CHRISTMAS, FOR ALWAYS

First North American Publication 2003

Copyright © 2003 by Caroline Anderson

This edition published by arrangement with Harlequin Books S.A.

® and TM are trademarks of the publisher. Trademarks indicated with
® are registered in the United States Patent and Trademark Office, the
Canadian Trade Marks Office and in other countries.

Visit us at www.eHarlequin.com

**Printed in U.S.A.**

# CHAPTER ONE

'WHAT on earth are you doing in my room?'

Oliver froze. It couldn't be. He was conjuring her up out of his miserable, fevered imagination because she'd been on his mind lately, but—Kate? *His* Kate? His heart and soul, the other half of himself, the part that made him whole?

He'd only just registered that the room was already occupied when he'd heard the bathroom door open behind him. Now he turned, his heart slamming against his ribs, and forced his mouth to smile. It was crooked, he could feel it, but his heart was trying to commit suicide and his legs were deserting him. He propped himself against the wall, the key swinging nonchalantly from his rigid fingers, and let his starving eyes rove hungrily over her.

She'd been in the shower. She was still wet, her fair hair clinging damply to her head, darkened by the water that even as he watched escaped and ran in a slow dribble down her neck and into the top of the towel.

The loose towel, the one she was hanging onto like grim death. The towel that hardly covered her. She'd hitched it up to cover her breasts, and all she'd achieved was hiking it higher on those glorious, endless legs that went all the way up...

'It's nice to see you, too,' he said, his voice roughened by the emotion rocking him.

'*Oliver?*' Kate swallowed, the slender column of

5

her throat working slightly with the action, and the dribble forked and ran down across the pale, smooth skin and pooled in the hollow of her clavicle.

His tongue ached to lick it, to flick out and gather the moisture on her skin and take it into his mouth. Would it taste of her?

'Oliver?' she said again, and he dragged his attention back to her face.

'Hello, Kate,' he said softly. 'How are you?'

'I'm fine—or I was,' she said, her voice scratchy. 'What are you doing in my room—and how did you get in here?'

He lifted the key, dangling it in front of her, and her brows pleated into a little frown.

'You've got a key?'

'Yes—and you shouldn't do that,' he told her, smoothing out the crease with his fingertip. 'You'll get lines.'

She scowled at him, hitching the towel closer as she stepped back, and he stifled a groan. Those legs...

'So who did you bribe?' she asked, her eyes wary behind the scowl.

'Bribe?'

'For the key. I'm sure you didn't come by it honestly.'

He felt one eyebrow rise. 'Is that any way to speak to your long-lost husband?' he chided.

'Ex-husband,' she corrected, but he shook his head.

'No—not unless I've missed something. You haven't ever got round to that, and I had no way of doing it, with no way to contact you.'

Her eyes slid away. 'So—who was it? The chambermaid? The porter? That pretty young thing on the desk?'

He gave a soft huff of laughter. 'I didn't *bribe* anyone, they just gave me the key. They must have had us both registered and got the names muddled. I take it you're here for the conference?'

She nodded, setting off another chain reaction with the rivulets of water, and he nearly groaned aloud.

'I'm sure there's a simple explanation,' he said, dragging his eyes away from her chest and sitting down on the end of the bed before his legs gave way. 'Why don't you phone down to Reception?'

'Yes, I will, since you're showing no signs of leaving. Perhaps they'll send someone to remove you,' she said, turning away. The phone was on the far side of the bed, and she knelt on the bed and reached across for it.

Foolish mistake. Her knee caught the hem of the towel as the mattress dipped, dragging it out of her hands. She scrabbled frantically for it as it fell, but it was too late. He'd seen her—seen the soft fullness of her breast, the hollow of her waist, the lush curve of her hip—and heat slammed through him.

'Ah, Katie...'

Their eyes locked, then her lids fluttered closed and she let out a soft wail of despair. 'Oliver, I don't need this,' she whispered.

'Need what?' he asked, his eyes skimming her shoulders, the smooth, pale skin that he knew would feel like silk under his hands. He reached out, running his fingers lightly over it, over the slender column of her throat, the pulse beating wildly under his fingertips.

'This?'

He turned his hand, brushing his knuckles over her

jaw, her chin, then reversing the action so his thumb dragged lightly over the soft, soft skin of her lips.

He felt the warm rush of breath as it left her body on a trembling sigh, and dropped his hand to cup her shoulder, gliding down to her elbow and then back up, round, down to where she held the towel in a death grip. His fingertips slipped behind the towel, the backs of his fingers following the delicate swell of her breast.

'Or this?' He could feel her chest rising and falling, her breathing rapid and shallow now in response to the adrenaline that must be coursing through her. It was certainly coursing through him.

He moved his hand down, the flat of his palm brushing over the fullness, bringing the nipple to attention. He felt it pebble under his hand, and closed his fingers over her, testing the weight, the fullness.

'Or this?' he whispered again.

'No...'

His hand moved on, over the curve of her hip, down to cup the swell of her bottom, then on, past the hem of the towel, to the firm skin of her thigh, chilled by the moisture drying on it. He could feel the goose-bumps, but was that the cold or his touch? Either. Both.

His hand moved again, and she gasped and pulled away, dragging the towel closer. 'Oliver, don't. I don't need this.'

'Liar,' he said softly.

'No!' she cried. She looked at him again pleadingly. 'No,' she repeated, more softly this time, but her eyes were giving him a different message, one he couldn't resist. 'Please—just go...'

But he couldn't. For five long years he'd ached for

her, and now she was here, gloriously naked under that inadequate towel and looking at him with those yearning, soft grey eyes, and he didn't have the strength to walk away.

'Not a chance,' he said gruffly, easing away from her and standing on legs that threatened to give way. He lost his jacket, ripped off his tie, gave up on the buttons and shredded the shirt before taking her in his arms.

'Oliver, no,' she moaned, but her lips were on his and they were saying yes, the fire hotter than ever, the need searing through him like molten steel. He heeled off his shoes, shucked off his trousers and briefs in one and gathered her into his arms.

Lord, she felt good. Her skin was cool and damp from her shower, and he took the towel from her hands and blotted her dry, following the towel with his lips, kissing every inch of that pale, translucent skin until it burned with the heat of his loving.

Her nipples pebbled, tight and puckered with the heat and the cold, and he drew first one, then the other into his mouth, stroking them tenderly, drawing on them while she cradled his head against her and gasped out his name.

'Oliver—please,' she whispered raggedly.

Please, what? Please, stop? Please, now?

He lifted his head and stared down into her eyes, and his breath jammed in his throat.

Her mouth was swollen and rosy from his kisses, her eyes wild with passion, and her hands were pleading with him.

How was he supposed to resist her?

\* \* \*

Kate couldn't believe it. Even while her body was still humming with the aftershocks of his love-making, her heart was breaking.

She must have been crazy. She should have marched over and yanked open the door and posted him through it—so why hadn't she?

The shock, she told herself. The shock of seeing him again after all these years, out of the blue like that. And all that studied nonchalance. She'd seen the pulse beating in his throat, seen the muscle jumping in his jaw, seen the need in his eyes—and she'd wanted him, too, feeble-minded and weak as she was.

She'd wanted him, and she'd had him, so now what?

She bit back the tears. What a fool she'd been to let him touch her. She should have thrown him out.

'Katie?'

'Don't call me that. Nobody calls me that now.'

'I do.'

'But I don't speak to you, so it doesn't matter,' she said, hardening her heart before it broke into a million pieces.

'That's not for want of trying on my part,' he said, his voice harsh now. 'What happened, Kate? One minute we were married, the next minute you'd left me with no more than a note that told me nothing, and I couldn't get hold of you. You'd left your job, quit the flat, your mother wouldn't tell me where you were—what did I do wrong, for God's sake? We were in love—or I was. I loved you, Kate. I still love you, dammit—but I have no idea why you left.'

She swung her legs over the edge of the bed, grabbing the towel now that it was too late and dragging it round herself ineffectually. 'You did nothing wrong. I just didn't love you any more,' she lied. 'We'd grown apart—changed. That's all.'

'And you couldn't tell me that, face to face?'

'I did—every time we had a row. It was no surprise.'

He gave a bitter laugh. 'It was to me.'

She reached for the phone, her hands shaking. 'I'm going to call Reception. You might like to get dressed,' she said, refusing to let herself look at his lean, sleek body with those taut muscles and the dark scatter of hair that she could still feel against her skin—

'Hello? This is Reception. Can I help you?'

How many times had the person spoken? She felt flags of colour run up her cheeks. 'This is Dr Crawford, in room 43. Dr Katharine Crawford. There seems to have been a mistake—you've given another key for my room to a Dr Oliver Crawford.'

'Oh. Hold on a moment, please,' the disembodied voice said, and she found herself connected to a hideous electronic rendition of 'Greensleeves'. She moved the phone away from her ear, but it was a mistake. All too clearly now, she could hear Oliver behind her, sighing harshly and then getting up, the bed dipping and jiggling as his weight shifted. Then she heard him unzipping a case, rummaging, the sound of him dressing...

'Hello? Dr Crawford, I'm so sorry, there appears to have been a mix-up. We do have another Dr Crawford registered, but he should be in room 44. We'll send someone up with the key now. I do apologise.'

The phone went dead before she could protest, and with a little shrug she cradled the receiver and looked down at the hand still clutching her towel in a futile and belated attempt at modesty.

It was too late for that—too late for all sorts of things.

No. Don't think about it. Don't go there.

'Katie?'

Oliver's voice was soft and yet gruff, and it was going to undo her if she allowed herself to listen to it. 'Oliver, no. We don't need a post-mortem—' she began, but he cut her off.

'I wasn't going to suggest it. I was just going to say, in the heat of the moment…we didn't think about contraception.'

Pain lanced through her, taking her breath away, and for a moment she said nothing, concentrating on the supposedly simple task of getting air into her lungs.

'Not necessary,' she said when she could speak, then added hastily, 'I'm on the Pill. Irregular periods—it tidies it up.'

He didn't reply. He was probably busy sorting through that one, working it out in his mind, testing it to see if he felt she was lying.

Which she was, of course, but he didn't need to know that and she'd deny it with her last breath. And if she couldn't get her lungs sorted out soon, that might be any minute—

A tap came on the door, saving them both from any further embarrassing revelations, and he went swiftly over to it and opened it just far enough to receive the key and the apology that came with it.

'Don't worry, no harm done,' he said with his usual easy charm, and she wondered how he could lie so fluently.

He came back to her, hefting the key in his hand and offering her a slightly crooked smile that didn't reach his eyes.

'Well, that's that sorted,' he said, and slipped the key into his pocket.

'Don't let me keep you,' she said, and he gave a heavy sigh.

'Kate, we need to talk.'

'There's nothing to say—'

His abrupt laugh cut her off. 'Nothing to say? We bump into each other for the first time in five years and go up in flames and there's *nothing to say*? Are you mad?'

'You thought so, five years ago.'

Something flickered in his eyes—something that could have been regret. 'No—I said you were acting strangely. And I was right. A week later you left me.'

'And that was strange? Hardly. As I've just told you, there was nothing between us any longer—and that hasn't changed.'

'Apparently not. There was nothing between us a moment ago,' he pointed out, deliberately twisting her words, and she looked away, unable to hold that steely grey gaze any longer. He had searching eyes, and they usually found what they were looking for. She couldn't risk that, not if she was going to keep her sanity and her resolve.

Not if she was going to let him go again.

'Oliver, please...'

She felt him move closer. 'The last time you said that, you were begging me to make love to you,' he murmured.

'In your dreams,' she said, getting to her feet and pushing past him. 'We've got this conference to get through. I'm sure we can manage to be civilised. Now, please, leave. I have to get ready for dinner. I'm starving, and I don't intend to miss it because of you.'

She heard his quiet sigh, then the sound of the zip on his case. 'I'll see you downstairs later,' he said, and it sounded like a promise. A moment later the door closed behind him with a deafening click, and she was alone.

Her legs gave way and she sat down abruptly on the floor.

A whole weekend to get through, with Oliver in the room next door and determined to talk to her. If she'd only known, she wouldn't have come here, she would have gone to another conference on something different.

*Then you wouldn't have seen him, wouldn't have made love with him again,* her alter ego whispered. *You wouldn't have felt his hands on you, the touch of his lips, the weight of his body—*

'Stop it!' she cried out, covering her ears, but the sounds were inside her and she couldn't shut them out. They were there, together with the memories of a love she'd thought could never die—a love she'd had to destroy to give him his freedom.

And now he was back in her life, however briefly, and she knew that if she slipped up even once, all the pain of the last few years would be in vain and the wounds would open up again, for them both.

She dragged in a breath, then another, and then got to her feet. She'd shower, to take the scent of him from her skin, and then she'd go down to dinner, and she'd be civil and ask him about his life and act like a friend.

*Liar! You just want to know what he's doing—if there's a woman in his life, if he's happy now. If he's got children...*

No. He wouldn't do that. Not without asking for a divorce and marrying the other woman. It wasn't his style.

But she could ask...

Kate was stunning—far and away the most beautiful woman in the room—and Oliver wasn't the only man to think so. Her long blonde hair was twisted up on the back of her head and held with wooden skewers that looked for all the world like chopsticks, and she was wearing a classic little black dress.

She looked calm and elegant and self-possessed, and he felt a moment of doubt. Had she moved on? Was that rubbish about the Pill and irregular periods true, or did she have a lover?

The thought burned like acid in his chest, and he breathed deeply and told himself not to be so stupid. She wouldn't do that—wouldn't sleep with him if there was another man in her life.

Would she? He didn't know. Once he'd been sure of her, but then it had all fallen suddenly and dramatically apart, and he'd realised he hadn't known her at all.

She saw him then, those strange pale grey eyes picking him out of the crowd with unerring accuracy, and without hesitation she crossed the room where they'd all gathered for the conference 'meet and greet', her smiling 'excuse me's parting the jostling hoards of delegates like a hot knife through butter.

Heads turned to follow her progress, and as she

reached his side he had a sudden, proprietorial urge to bend down and kiss her thoroughly on the lips.

He'd be banging his chest next and dragging her off to his tree house, he thought with disgust, and forced himself to behave. He couldn't help the hand that came to rest on the curve of her spine, though, as they made their way through the crowd to a quieter corner.

He snagged two glasses of wine off a passing waiter, and ushered her to a little sofa tucked away beside a log fire. He handed her a glass. 'Hope white's OK?'

'Fine. Thank you.' She sipped it almost absently, leaving a faint curve of delicate rose against the glass where her lip had touched it...

Damn. He had to stop thinking about her lips. Instead, he studied her thoughtfully, trying to see the changes that had to be there after five years. He drew a blank. If there were any changes, they were so minute he couldn't see them. She might have been a little finer drawn, and he had a feeling that she was tired, but otherwise she was still his Kate, the woman he'd fallen in love with over eight years ago.

She set the glass down and looked up, her eyes meeting his with a challenge. She seemed wary, for all her self-possession, and it dawned on him he might owe her an apology.

They spoke simultaneously, then smiled, the ice breaking a little.

'You go first,' she said, so he tried again.

'About earlier,' he began, and he could sense her withdrawal. Tough. She'd told him to go first, and she was going to hear him out. 'I'd only been in your room long enough to realise that it was occupied when you came out of the shower. I honestly had no idea it was your room until I saw you, and I certainly didn't plan...'

He faltered, not sure how to describe the amazing and unexpected joy of making love to her.

She looked away, and only the faint run of colour over her cheeks gave away her feelings. 'It's all right, I do believe you. It was just one of those things.'

'So you'll forgive me?'

She hesitated so long his heart sank, but then she straightened her shoulders and turned back to him, and her eyes were curiously expressionless.

'I'm going to forget it ever happened,' she said, 'and I'd like you to do the same.'

Not a chance. Not a single chance in the world that he could forget making love to her again, forget her wild, uninhibited response, forget the small, frantic noises she'd made...

Oliver shifted on the seat, looking away from those expressionless eyes. When had she learned to do that? He used to be able to read every thought in her head. She must have started playing poker.

'We'll have to agree to differ on that,' he said gruffly, 'but if I promise not to mention it, will that do?' He dredged up a smile, but if it was as strained as hers, it wasn't very convincing.

Kate shrugged. 'It'll have to. We're stuck with this situation for the weekend. We'll just have to make the best of it.' She straightened, picked up her glass, threw him another tight smile. 'So—tell me about yourself. What are you doing now?'

How could he be so relaxed? He was slouched against the corner of the sofa, one arm draped along the back so he was turned half-towards her. His wineglass was balanced against his belt buckle, half-dangling from those long, strong fingers that knew her so well...

No. She wasn't going to think about that. Kate forced herself to concentrate on what he was saying.

'Wanted a partner in the practice, so I took it on. I've been there three years now, and it's good.'

'Where is it?' she asked, wondering if he'd already given her that information, and he probably had because, instead of giving her the name of a town or village, he just said, 'Halfway up the hill on the left, where it always was—you know, next to the undertaker and two doors down from the florist. You'll remember the jokes about the location.'

The penny dropped. She'd seen the old surgery many times when they'd been visiting his parents—had even used the surgery once, for a throat infection—and now he was working there, apparently, in Gippingham, the little market town that he called home. She should have realised. He'd always talked about going back to his roots.

'I remember it being rather quaint and old-fashioned,' she said slowly, still assimilating the information, and he laughed.

'That's the one. It's been extended since Peter Abraham became senior partner, but it still reminds me of going to the doctor when I was a child. It was in there that I realised I wanted to be a doctor—well, not just a doctor, a GP, but, of course, in those days I didn't know there was any other kind of doctor. I was only seven or so at the time.'

She could picture him in the photographs his mother had showed her, all gangly arms and legs and gappy smile. She'd thought at the time how wonder-

ful it would be to have a son like him, never
dreaming—

No.

She leant back in the corner of the sofa, swirling
her wine absently, shutting down that corner of her
mind.

'So you've gone home. You always said you
would. I expect your parents are pleased.'

His face shadowed and he dropped his eyes. 'My
mother is. My father's dead—two years ago. He had
a heart attack when he was milking. My mother went
looking for him when he didn't come in for breakfast.
And, of course, I was on call. He was gone when I
got there—probably died instantly.'

She reached out to him without thinking, resting
her hand on his leg in a gesture of comfort. 'Oliver,
I'm so sorry. It must have been dreadful.'

He looked up at her then, his lips twisting into a
wry, crooked smile that didn't reach his eyes, and he
took her hand in his and squeezed it gently.

'It was tough to accept at first, but on post-mortem
they found a tumour on one of his lungs, so really he
was lucky. If he'd lived, it would have been much
worse before it was over.' He patted her hand and
straightened up, putting the subject away. 'So—what
about you?' he asked, his voice soft. 'You were going
into paediatrics—I didn't think you were interested in
general practice.'

Kate shrugged and leant back, easing her hand
away from his before she got too used to the warmth
and familiarity of the simple gesture. 'I changed my
mind,' she said simply, leaving out all the painful
realisations that had been part of the decision-making
process.

'Paeds is hard,' he said. 'I couldn't do it—watching the kids die—and I would have been surprised if you could.'

She didn't bother to correct him. It would have opened a whole new can of worms.

'I've been working in East Anglia, north east Suffolk mainly, but then my grandmother was taken ill and needed looking after, so I moved up to Norfolk and lived with her, doing locum jobs when she was well enough. She died in September, and I'm still deciding what to do, where to go next.'

'My turn to commiserate,' he said quietly. 'I never met your grandmother, but I know how fond you were of her. I'm sorry you had to go through that. What was it in the end?'

'Just old age. Her body was worn out. Nothing wrong with her mind, though. She was as sharp as a tack.' And she'd given Kate hell, on a daily basis, for leaving Oliver.

'Stupid girl. You should have given him the choice,' she'd said, over and over again, and it had made her wonder. Maybe now she'd met him again she could reassess the situation.

Or not. Silly idea. Her grandmother, much as she'd loved her, had been wrong about this. She'd never known him, hadn't realised how important family was to him. Kate did, though—and anyway, it might be too late, for all she knew. There could be someone else.

'So—who's the woman in your life now?' she asked brightly, changing the subject to one she was much more interested in in a masochistic way.

Something flickered in his eyes, and he laughed softly and set down his glass.

'After what happened earlier, you have to ask me that?' he said, his voice slightly rough at the edges.

With emotion? Or desire?

Oh, lord. She took a gulp of her wine and put the glass down. 'We weren't going to talk about that.'

'So we weren't. Sorry.' He smiled, looking utterly unrepentant, and she could have screamed.

She was rescued from the situation by the conference organiser, standing on a chair and calling for their attention.

'Good evening, ladies and gentlemen. I'd like to welcome you all here to Aldeburgh for what I hope is going to be a very busy and productive weekend. As you know, our subject is the care of the well woman in general practice, and we've planned a very full programme for you, starting after dinner tonight with a brief introduction to the seminars we've laid on for you tomorrow. Following that, the rest of the evening is your own, and I hope you enjoy it. Now, I'm sure you'll be pleased to know that the buffet is ready, if you'd like to make your way through to the restaurant.'

'Saved by the bell,' Oliver murmured, and she flushed. He might have had the grace to let the subject drop, but that would have been too much to ask.

'I suppose we ought to circulate—talk to other doctors, sound them out on their views,' she said, getting to her feet, but he wasn't that easily despatched.

'You could sound me out on my views. Do you know, for example, my opinion on breast screening? Or emergency contraception? Or HRT in symptomless menopausal women? And look on the bright side—if I get boring, you can always tell me to shut up.'

Boring? Oliver? Not in a million years.

'What a good idea,' she said blithely, setting her glass down on the table and picking up her bag. 'I'll bear it in mind.'

'I don't doubt it,' he murmured, following altogether too close behind her, so that she was utterly aware of him, of the warmth of his body, the subtle scent of his aftershave, dry and citrusy with a warm hint of musk. It hadn't been so obvious when they'd been sitting down, but now, as they all crowded together around the doorway to the restaurant, it surrounded her and brought memories flooding back.

Memories she would rather have left alone, of tender, intimate moments—going out in the evening to parties, dancing together, their bodies snugly aligned from head to toe, then going home and finishing what they'd started...

'Penny for them.'

'You'd be overcharged,' she said lightly. 'I was just woolgathering.'

Kate dragged her thoughts back into order and went through to the restaurant. She didn't want to be with him, didn't want all these constant reminders of what she couldn't have, so she turned to him once she'd filled her plate and met those intelligent, searching grey eyes full on.

'Why don't we circulate—independently?' she suggested.

For a moment Oliver said nothing, then he dropped a scoop of pasta salad on his plate, tossed the spoon back in the dish and shrugged.

'If that's what you want.'

And he turned on his heel and walked away, disappearing into the crowd of delegates and circulating, as she'd suggested, with ridiculous ease.

She was suddenly alone, and for a moment she felt utterly lost. She was a fool. It was only one weekend—it might be the only weekend in the rest of her life she got to spend time with him. Why throw it away?

'Hi, I'm Graham.'

She found a hand thrust at her, but she had a plate in one hand and a glass in the other, so she just shrugged and laughed apologetically.

'Sorry. Hands full. I'm Kate.'

'Is he a friend of yours?'

Her eyes tracked instinctively to Oliver. Was he a friend? Her best friend in the world, once. A lover—certainly that again, as of a few short hours ago. A husband—but not any more, and not ever again, to her great regret. She wasn't ready to share any of it with this stranger.

'He used to be.'

The bitterness and regret must have shown in her voice, because Graham winced. 'Ouch. Sounds painful and messy.'

'It is. I'd rather not talk about it. What about you? Any painful, messy parts of your life you don't want to discuss?'

He winced again and gave her an apologetic smile. '*Touché*. I'm sorry. I'm obviously treading on some very fragile eggshells, but for a moment there, you seemed a little abandoned. I thought you might need help.'

She looked at him then—really looked at him, for the first time—and saw kindness and understanding and, yes, pain in his eyes. He was wearing a wedding ring, and he seemed safe.

'I'm sorry,' she said, relenting. 'He's my ex-husband. I didn't expect to see him here.'

'I wondered. I've been watching you—you didn't look comfortable. I thought he might be harassing you.'

She shook her head. 'No. He's just…here.'

Graham's eyes clouded. 'Be grateful for that. I'll never see my wife again. I lost her last year—cancer. Damn, I wasn't going to talk about it—'

He broke off, his eyes a little too bright, and Kate's heart reached out to him. He was a nice man—probably a good doctor—and he was lonely.

'Then let's not. Let's talk about this conference. What are your opinions on emergency contraception?'

He stared at her blankly for a second, then laughed. 'I don't know that I have any.'

She gave him a brilliant smile. 'Then why don't we find a seat before I starve to death standing here holding this lot, and we can explore our opinions in comfort?'

'What a good idea,' he said, and led the way towards a vacant table.

She followed him, but she couldn't help glancing over her shoulder as they crossed the room, searching for that dark head and those piercing steel-grey eyes that she felt sure were watching her.

They were looking very cosy.

Oliver didn't know who the hell the guy was, but he was laughing with Kate and leaning towards her, hanging on her every word, and he was ready to punch the man's lights out.

Idiot. It was nothing to do with him. She wasn't his any more.

She had been, though, just a few hours ago.

Would she sleep with that man tonight?

Pain ripped through him, catching him unawares, and he excused himself from the conversation and made his way across the room to the french doors. He went out into the garden, dragging in lungfuls of the bracing sea air and telling himself it was none of his business who Kate slept with.

Even if she had just made love with him only this evening.

For all he knew she was involved in a relationship with someone else now. Maybe that was why she was on the Pill, and it was nothing to do with her periods. The irregular cycle thing made sense, of course, because she'd had that when they'd still been living together, but it needn't be the only reason she was taking it. And if she wasn't in a relationship, maybe it just gave her an element of sexual freedom.

'Oh, you fool, you shouldn't have touched her,' he muttered, resting his head against a pillar and staring out over the dark garden. He had, though, and he couldn't regret it, even if it would eat him alive watching her for the rest of the evening laughing with that man.

He couldn't do it. He was going up to bed—to the room next to hers, so he'd hear her come in, hear their voices, their laughter, the sounds of their love-making...

Unless she went to his room.

Oliver went back inside abruptly, and found the man ensconced in a group, involving himself in an animated discussion about a GP who was being sued by a female patient in a hail of publicity.

There was no sign of Kate.

Fingering the key in his pocket, he contemplated staying up a little longer, but he felt restless and edgy, and he wanted to be alone.

That was a lie. He wanted to be with Kate, but it wasn't going to happen. It was a lousy idea anyway. She'd torn him apart five years ago, and only an idiot would expose himself to another opportunity for more of the same.

The introduction to the seminars was over, there was no need to stay down here and torture himself any further. He went upstairs, hesitated outside her room and then went on to the next door and let himself in.

Seconds later there was a tap on the door, and he opened it warily. Kate was standing there, her eyes hesitant.

'Hi,' he murmured, then waited.

For a moment he thought she was going to run away, but then she straightened her shoulders and firmed that soft, mobile mouth.

'I wondered…if you fancied a coffee. I've put the kettle on.'

Coffee was the last thing on his mind, but if it gave him time with her…

'That would be good,' he said, and, ignoring the nagging voice that told him he was a fool, he picked up his key, flicked off the light and followed her.

# CHAPTER TWO

SHE must be crazy. Why on earth had she invited him in for coffee? She had no idea what she was going to say to him but, after hearing the pain in Graham's voice when he'd talked about his wife, she just knew she couldn't let the weekend pass without spending as much of it with Oliver as she could.

What if it should be her last chance to be alone with him? Even if he didn't have a woman in his life now—and he still hadn't answered that to her satisfaction—it didn't mean he wouldn't, and if she did nothing else, she wanted to spend part of this weekend achieving closure, so they could both move on with their lives.

So Kate led him into her room, gave him what she hoped passed for a smile and waved at the chair by the window.

'Have a seat. It won't be a moment, these little kettles don't take long.'

'I don't want coffee.'

Her mouth opened to speak, then she met his eyes and her breath hitched in her throat.

He was standing close to her, just inches away, and as their eyes locked and held, he lifted one hand and pulled the wooden skewers out of her hair, releasing it. She felt it fall around her shoulders, and then he threaded his fingers through it, sifting it in his hands, smoothing it back from her face with the pad of his thumb.

He was going to kiss her. She knew that, just as she knew the sun would rise in the morning, and she was as powerless to stop it. He lowered his head, his eyes still locked with hers, and then his lids fluttered down and his mouth found hers and settled, soft and warm and coaxing.

She closed her eyes, leaning into him with a little whimper of need and resignation, and his arms tightened around her, easing her closer, cradling her against his chest. She could feel his heart pounding— or was it hers?

Both, probably. It didn't matter. Nothing mattered except the fact that she was in his arms.

And she shouldn't be. She pressed her hands on his chest, pushing slightly, and he lifted his head just far enough to look down into her eyes.

'What's wrong?'

'This. Us. Everything. This isn't why I asked you in here.'

He searched her eyes, and with a quiet sigh he let her go.

'Why did you?'

Kate shrugged and turned away, crossing to the kettle to give herself room. 'I wanted to talk to you,' she said. 'To be friends. Does that sound crazy?'

Oliver's laugh was strained. 'Friends? Yeah, it sounds crazy. Talking about our divorce would make more sense.'

'Divorce?' Did she sound as stunned as she felt? She hadn't even given it a thought, but Oliver obviously had. 'Is that what you want?' she asked him, her voice not as steady as she would have liked.

'I don't think this is about me. It wasn't me that left, out of the blue, without warning—'

'Hardly without warning! We were fighting like cat and dog. It wasn't working.'

'It was a tough time for us. We were working apart, commuting for the weekends—it was awful. Of course it wasn't working. We just needed to sit it out, but you couldn't see that, couldn't give us that chance, and you didn't even have the grace to talk about it.'

She swallowed, wondering how near the truth she could go. 'We weren't doing each other any favours,' she said carefully. 'You needed things I couldn't give you, and so we were fighting all the time.'

'I remember. I also remember making up.'

His voice was deep and husky, and it sent shivers through her. Making up had always been the best part of their arguments, but in the end it couldn't solve their one insurmountable problem, the thing that had driven them apart. It had simply brought it home to her even harder.

'Whatever. I just wanted to know that you're all right,' she said, refusing to be dragged down that particular blind alley.

His laugh was harsh. 'Do you really care? You didn't earlier. You wanted to circulate independently, as I recall, but I didn't notice you doing much circulating—not once you met up with your charmingly attentive companion.'

He sounded bitter. Or jealous. How odd. He'd never been the possessive type, he'd always trusted her before—but she'd destroyed his trust, his faith in her, and even though she'd had no choice, she was shocked at how much that hurt.

'Graham's a nice man,' she said defensively, and Oliver's mouth curled into a derisive smile.

'I'm sure. I'm glad you had a *nice* evening. Now, if you'll excuse me, I'm really very tired and I don't need an update on your sexual conquests. I'll see you at breakfast—if you aren't still tied up with your nice friend Graham.'

Shock held Kate rigid for a moment. 'What are you implying?'

'You're supposed to be clever—you work it out,' he growled.

'How *dare* you!'

'Why shouldn't I dare? You slept with me at the drop of a towel—'

'And what an error of judgement that was turning out to be! Well, never again!'

'Fine—just so long as we both know where we stand,' he snarled, and, wrenching the door open, he stalked out.

She followed him, standing right behind him in the corridor, not ready to let it go.

'What have I ever done to make you suggest I'd do such a thing, anyway?' she demanded. 'You know me better than that.'

'Do I?' For a fleeting second his eyes were raw with pain. 'I used to think I did, but I'm not so sure any more,' he said, and, going into his room, he closed the door.

She swallowed hard and turned back to her room, to find that in her absence her door had quietly swung to and shut. She was locked out on the landing in her stockinged feet, and the only way she could get back in was to go down to Reception and get another key.

'Oh, *hell*!' she muttered, and biting back tears of rage and humiliation, she took a deep breath and went downstairs.

*    *    *

The first seminar was on screening. It was important, and relevant, but the statistics on detection rates and errors and recalls for both breast and cervical screening were as dry as dust and couldn't hold Kate's attention.

She hadn't seen Oliver at breakfast, but that might have been because she'd tossed and turned all night and finally gone to sleep at four, still horribly aware of him in the room next door, and been so late she'd only just caught the tail end of breakfast. She'd grabbed a quick cup of coffee and a bowl of cereal, and now she felt gritty-eyed and restless.

The seminar ground to a halt, and she went out into the hotel lounge for coffee. Maybe it would wake her up, she thought, and with any luck she'd be able to creep quietly into a corner and drink it undisturbed.

No such luck. She turned, cup in hand, to find Graham beside her.

'Morning. That was interesting, wasn't it?' he said, reaching past her for a biscuit.

'I wasn't really concentrating,' she said, wondering how she could excuse herself. OK, he was nice, but just then she didn't want nice, she wanted solitude.

Her opportunity to escape came all too suddenly, in the guise of Oliver. Not what she would have planned at all, but he walked straight up to them and, without sparing Graham a glance, he said, 'May I have a quick word?'

She turned to Graham, an excuse forming on her lips, but he just smiled. 'Don't worry, take your time. I've just seen someone else I want to catch up with anyway.'

He squeezed Kate's elbow, just a little touch for

reassurance, and she turned her eyes back to Oliver reluctantly.

'What is it?' she asked with very little grace. Frankly, after the way he'd behaved the night before she didn't feel grace was exactly necessary, but he didn't look put out by her abruptness. In fact, if anything, he looked a little embarrassed.

'It's about last night.'

'Your behaviour was totally uncalled-for.'

'That's my line,' he said, one corner of his mouth lifting in a wry smile. The smile slipped again, gone as quickly as it had come, and he looked down at the cup in his hand, giving it unwarranted attention for a moment.

'I'm really sorry,' he said finally. 'I don't know what came over me, making a crack like that. All I can say is I wasn't thinking with my head—not at all, from the moment I first set eyes on you in your room when I arrived, but you would have had to have changed beyond recognition to behave like that, and I can't believe I suggested it. And you're right. We ought to be friends. We always used to be. We could be again—if you'll give me another chance?'

She would have spoken, but there was a lump the size of her fist lodged in her throat, and his face started to swim in front of her eyes.

'Ah, hell, Katie,' he murmured, and, taking her elbow—the other one—he led her away from the crowd and round the corner to the sofa by the fire that they'd found the night before.

'I'm fine,' she said, blinking away the stupid, stupid tears. 'Apology accepted.'

'I tried to deliver it last night, but you wouldn't open your door.'

She gave him a rueful smile. 'I probably wasn't there. I locked myself out—when I followed you. I didn't take my key—I hate those self-closing doors. I had to go down to Reception and beg a spare.'

'That would explain it. I tried this morning, as well, when I came back from breakfast, but I could hear your shower running and I didn't thinking knocking on your door was a good idea, bearing in mind how I tend to react to you under those circumstances.'

A warm tide of colour ran up her throat, and she made a noncommittal noise and concentrated on her coffee for a moment.

Oliver leant back in into the corner of the sofa again, one foot crossed over the other knee, his cup balanced on the arm of the sofa. 'So, what did you think of this morning's contribution?'

'Quite interesting.'

'You have to be joking! It was as boring as hell. I hate statistics.'

Kate gave a soft chuckle and met his eyes. 'So do I. Nevertheless, it was probably all very useful information. I wish I'd paid a bit more attention now. Still, what have we got after coffee?' she asked him.

'Dilemmas in contraception,' he said. 'The Q and A after that should be quite interesting. I expect at all sorts of ethical issues will be raised, particularly in relation to emergency contraception and teenagers under age. I had a 14-year-old last week who wanted the morning-after pill. It's the third time she's come in, and I'm beginning to wonder if I shouldn't involve her parents.'

'Tricky.'

'Absolutely. I don't want to betray her trust, but on the other hand I don't want her relying on it as a form of contraception and it doesn't always work, of course. My sister-in-law, Julia, is living proof of that. She's pregnant with their fifth child.'

What a twist of fate. She struggled for a sensible remark. 'Good heavens. They only had two when I knew them.'

'Yeah, well, they've been busy! She's due in about five weeks, and of course they're delighted now, but I gave Stephen a fairly hard time about behaving like a teenager—and here I am,' he added, his voice low, 'doing exactly the same thing with you, without giving contraception a second thought.'

'Except, of course, I'm not going to get pregnant,' she said, ruthlessly putting away the pain. 'So, we've got dilemmas in contraception before lunch, and what about after lunch?'

'Antenatal care, then tea, and then the role of HRT in the menopause and premature ovarian failure.'

Her cup rattled in her saucer and she put it down abruptly on the little table. 'Lots of material there, then,' she said lightly, and wondered why on earth she hadn't read the literature more closely, and why she'd chosen to come on this course instead of all the many others she could have selected as part of her required and ongoing vocational training.

The fact was, of course, it was highly relevant to her role as a woman doctor, and that was why she'd chosen it. Since she was going to be in general practice, she would automatically be working with a lot of women. She'd always known she would have to learn to deal with that. It was just that sitting here, next to Oliver, made it somehow all so much harder.

So much more relevant, somehow, than when she was living and working as a single woman. She could handle it then. It was easy, in a way, firmly in the background.

Now, though—now it was up close and personal, and she didn't know how she was going to get through that particular seminar with Oliver at her side, without him realising something was wrong.

And that, of course, was something she had to avoid at all costs. If he ever got wind of why she'd left him, then being the man he was he'd be so busy doing the decent thing that he wouldn't do what was right for him, and then he'd never have the children he longed for.

It didn't matter that she couldn't have them. She would have liked them, sure, but she could live without. Oliver, though, had talked about nothing else but starting their family, and he was wonderful with children.

He'd be a brilliant father. She couldn't deny him the right to that, and she could think of nothing worse than being trapped in a marriage with him and watching her childlessness eat him alive.

And it would. When her premature ovarian failure had been diagnosed, she'd been trying to summon up the courage to tell him, but before she could do so, he'd come back at the weekend from the practice where he'd been training and told her about a woman of twenty-five who'd just been given the same devastating diagnosis.

'Can you imagine? She's twenty-five, Katie, and she's all washed up. She can't have kids, she's going to be an old woman before her time. And the worst of it is she's still single. She hasn't even found the man she wants to spend her life with, and she's got nothing to offer. It's so sad—life's really cruel sometimes. Poor woman—who's going to want her?'

Who, indeed? Not him, clearly. She could still hear the pity in his voice, see the look on his face. Somehow she'd struggled through the weekend, and then on the Monday she'd called in sick, taken the few things she'd felt were exclusively hers and had gone to her grandmother's.

The only other person in the world she'd told had been her mother, and for the last five years she'd fielded Oliver's questions and returned his letters and defended her daughter's privacy with all the courage and dedication of a lioness with cubs.

'It should be a good day,' Oliver was saying.

Kate stared at him blankly for a second, then her brain clicked back into gear. 'I'll see how it goes,' she said. 'I'm tired—a bit spaced out. I didn't sleep very well. I hate strange beds. I might have to bottle out by then.'

For a moment she thought he was going to say something, but then he just smiled and nodded, and turned his attention back to his coffee.

Something was wrong.

Oliver had no idea what, but she looked…drained, really. More tired than he'd realised. Her grandmother's death had probably taken it out of her and, knowing Kate, she would have got involved in every moment of the woman's terminal care.

That could be very demanding, both physically and emotionally, and was probably all that was wrong.

That and bumping into him again. That in itself might have been quite a shock, and he hadn't made it exactly easy for her, starting with jumping her bones and ending with the uncalled-for tongue-lashing he'd given her last night.

He gave a quiet sigh and put his cup down. 'Time to go and face the dilemmas of contraception. You feeling up to it?'

She smiled, her eyes a little bright, and stood up. 'Ready when you are.'

Oliver had been right. There was a lively discussion in the question-and-answer session after the contra-ception seminar, and the discussion continued through lunch, relieving Kate of the necessity of finding any-thing else to say.

Graham cornered her at one point, his eyes worried. 'Everything OK?'

'Fine,' she lied, dredging up a smile. 'Don't worry about me, I'm all right.'

'Well, I'm here if you need a shoulder.'

She thanked him, all too conscious of Oliver's eyes on her across the room, and excusing herself she made her way back to him.

'All right?' he asked softly.

'Do I look as if I'm on the verge of a crisis?' she asked him with a smile. 'Graham just asked me that.'

Oliver's answering smile was tight. 'You obviously bring out the protective instinct in all your men.'

Kate gave a startled laugh. 'All my men? Are we back to that again?'

His smile this time was rueful. 'Sorry. I didn't mean it to sound like that. Have you had all you want to eat? If so, I think there's some coffee in the lounge.'

'Coffee sounds good,' she replied, and, after col-lecting their cups, they joined another lively ethical discussion. Well, to be exact, she joined the discussion, waited until Oliver became involved, as she'd known he would, and then retreated into silence.

That had two advantages. The first was that she didn't have to try and think of anything intelligent to say, no mean achievement on an almost total lack of sleep, and the second was that she could watch Oliver.

He talked, she thought with an inward smile, with his whole body. Twice his coffee nearly slopped over into the saucer, and his expression became intense and animated. He was totally focused on the discussion, as he became focused on everything he did, and as she stood there, watching and listening to him, she fell in love with him all over again.

Not that she'd ever fallen out of love—more talked herself out of it, to preserve her sanity, and the man she'd fallen in love with eight years ago could have been quite different now.

He hadn't changed, though. He'd just become more so. More dynamic, more intense, more witty, his mind even more razor sharp, and the planes and angles of his face were, if anything, even more attractive.

Kate watched his lips, mobile and expressive, and remembered the feel of them last night, soft and persuasive. It would have been so easy...

She dragged herself back to the conversation. It was getting more and more heated, and one man who she'd already labelled as a bigot announced abruptly, 'Well, I think it's all totally unnecessary anyway. People should be able to control themselves.'

Oliver's eyes sparkled with mischief. 'Oh, come on. Haven't you ever been overtaken by a wild and spontaneous urge?'

The bigot straightened in affront. 'Certainly not,' he replied, and Oliver smiled.

She recognised that smile. It spelt danger, and her heart sank. 'In which case,' he went on, 'my heart bleeds for you—but, then, of course, you're not married to my wife.'

He turned the smile on Kate, ignoring her tiny gasp of protest, and pressed a quick and no doubt harmless kiss to her lips. Well, harmless to her anyway, but she was incensed, and so she bit him.

Not hard enough to draw blood, but hard enough to make him pull back, his eyes widening in surprise. Then he grinned again, slung an arm casually round her shoulders and steered her away, leaving the others chuckling behind them.

'That wasn't nice,' he murmured.

'Nor was the stunt you pulled. You were strutting like a cockerel.'

'Cock-a-doodle-do,' he said softly in her ear. How on earth could he make something like that sound seductive? She glared at him.

'It was unnecessary.'

'Nonsense. I couldn't let that idiot get away with it any longer. Pompous ass. He deserved to be taken down a peg or two.'

'You didn't have to use me to do it,' she pointed out, but he was totally unabashed.

'Lighten up,' he ordered. 'The man's an idiot.'

'It must be something to do with that Y chromosome,' she retorted, and wondered how she could have thought she was in love with him still.

And then he smiled at her, that rueful, wicked little smile that won her round every time, and she melted all over again.

'Forgive me,' he said, still utterly unrepentant, and she laughed.

'You don't deserve it.'

She realised the others were drifting off, and it dawned on her that it was time for the next session.

'We ought to go back in. What is it now?'

'Antenatals,' he said, and she nodded.

'Of course. I forgot,' she said, although it wasn't that so much as failing to register because of dreading what was coming afterwards. She still wasn't sure she could attend the HRT lecture, and yet what would arouse more suspicion, ducking out of the session or her reaction to it? Because she wasn't sure she could hide her reaction from Oliver, of all people.

To start laying the foundations for her escape route, she manufactured a yawn, and he frowned down at her.

'You really are tired,' he said softly.

'I said so.'

'I could help you rest.'

Kate snorted and headed for the door, ignoring his teasing and suggestive remark. 'Help like that I can do without,' she replied, taking a handout from the person at the door and heading for a vacant seat.

'Just a suggestion,' he murmured, settling into the chair beside her.

He was close—too close, probably deliberately, and she knew she would miss every word. She shifted so that she was slightly further away from him, and then, forcing herself to pay attention, she studied the antenatal handout as if her life depended on it.

'Premature ovarian failure isn't as rare as people imagine.'

Tell me about it, thought Kate. She'd decided to

tough it out and attend the dreaded last lecture of the day, but now she was there she was regretting it. She schooled her expression and concentrated on taking notes. Totally unnecessary, but it kept her mind busy and her head down, which was ideal.

'Don't underestimate the impact of your diagnosis on the woman and her family,' the lecturer said, and if it hadn't been so true and so bitterly familiar, Kate would have laughed out loud. 'And don't forget that it doesn't only affect fertility. There are many reasons why women's ovaries fail prematurely, plunging them into an early menopause, and eliminating underlying disease should of course be one of your objectives.'

He went over the things that could trigger it, and then went on to discuss the problems a woman with POF could face, such as increased risk of osteoporosis, heart disease, colon cancer, Alzheimer's, Parkinson's, diabetes—the list was long and horribly familiar to Kate, and of course the earlier the ovarian failure, the greater the risk. She'd been twenty-five—and she'd still needed that oestrogen desperately for her health, never mind her fertility and her emotional stability and self-esteem.

Beside her Oliver shifted, and she felt a great wave of regret. He was so unconsciously masculine, so male to her female—but her femininity was just a sham, a hollow shell worn out before its time. Self-pity, she thought in disgust, and turned her attention back to the speaker.

'On the handout is a checklist of symptoms, many of which are the same as for the normally menopausal woman, but there are other pointers such as family history of pituitary problems, deafness, autoimmune disorder and so on. Get your patient to make a diary to throw up any pattern of bleeding, moodiness, temperature fluctuation, night sweats and any other unusual things. Do a pregnancy test, thyroid and pituitary tests and look again at autoimmune disorders.

'The primary diagnostic tool, however, is the FSH level. If the follicle stimulating hormones are significantly elevated, it's an almost sure indicator of ovarian failure.'

Yup, she thought. That was me. Oh, lord, I could take this lecture with my eyes shut and my hands tied behind my back. Why am I here?

But he talked about HRT, about the dangers as well as the advantages, brought them up to speed on current thinking and made several useful suggestions, so it wasn't in vain, and it wouldn't last for ever. He'd be winding up soon, she told herself.

All she had to do was get through it.


Oliver frowned slightly, watching as Kate wrote down endless notes. Surely that lot was contained in the handout? Perhaps she hadn't looked at it, or maybe it was an area she felt unsure of. Strange. She hadn't made notes in any of the other seminars.

Oh, well. He gave a mental shrug and flexed his shoulders. He was ready for a break, and if it wasn't dark already he would have liked to have gone for a walk. Perhaps he would anyway. The streets around the hotel were all well lit, and he might take a stroll along the seafront. Maybe Kate would come too.

And maybe he needed some time away from her to get his thoughts in order. Seeing her again had brought back all the memories of their time together, both good and bad, although the bad were heavily outnumbered. Those memories needed sifting through and filing again, and he needed to come to terms with the idea that she was going to be out of his life again in just a few short hours.

It was so tempting—horribly, overwhelmingly tempting—to try and convince her to spend the night with him, but he didn't think it was fair. He was sure that if he put his mind to it he could talk her into it, but he didn't want her like that.

Oh, liar, sure you do, his alter ego jeered, but he knew he didn't, not in his heart of hearts. He wanted her, of course he did, but only if she wanted him, too, in equal measure.

The lecturer was winding up, and he turned to Kate and caught a bleak look in her eyes before she hastily turned away. Was she feeling as sad about leaving him tomorrow as he was about leaving her? In which case...

'I'm going up for a rest now,' she said, standing up and making a production of gathering her things together.

Oliver stood, meaning to escort her to her room, but he was intercepted by an old friend, and by the time he'd got away, there was no sign of her. In fact she managed to avoid him for the rest of the day, pointedly eating her dinner in the company of the very nice Graham, which made him grind his teeth.

He must have imagined that sadness. Probably Kate was just tired, or thinking about her grandmother. Sometimes his father would come to mind out of the blue, and the grief would catch him unawares.

Yes, that was it, nothing to do with him at all. He was deluding himself if he thought she was. She wasn't sorry to be seeing the back of him, far from it. She probably couldn't wait to get away.

He pushed his food around his plate, got involved in a heated discussion, probably had more wine than was good for him, and went to bed.

Kate went down early for breakfast. She'd seen Oliver embroiled in a very lively argument the night before, all of them somewhat the worse for wear, and she had a feeling he wouldn't be up too early.

She was wrong. He was there, looking fresh as a daisy and obviously just out of the shower, his hair still damp and a plate heaped with the fullest English breakfast she'd seen in a long time squatting on the table in front of him.

He threw her a grin. 'Join me.'

'And look at that lot?' she said, raising a brow, but she did join him because she hated eating on her own and, nice though he might be, Graham was getting a bit wearing.

'You're looking revoltingly chipper this morning,' she told him, and he laughed.

'Nothing like a good greasy breakfast after a heavy night,' he said, stabbing a mushroom and eating it with relish. Her stomach quivered at the thought, and when the waiter came over to her, she ordered her usual breakfast.

'Cereal and toast?' he said in disgust. 'You'll fade away.'

'Which is probably better than the alternative,' she retorted, and dived into her bran flakes. 'So, what's on the menu today, conference-wise?'

'Well-woman checks, obstetric emergencies and postnatal depression.'

Kate heaved an inward sigh of relief. She could cope with all of those. Even the obstetrics, which she had thought would be hard, was, in fact, just an interesting part of her job. Relaxing, she finished her breakfast, smiled at Graham across the room and settled back with her coffee.

Oliver set down his knife and fork at last and looked up at her, studying her closely. 'So—what are you doing next, after you leave here?'

She shrugged. 'I don't know. I expect I'll find another job. I've registered for locum work in Norfolk obviously, but I'm still registered in East Suffolk because of my previous job. I'll have to see.'

He nodded thoughtfully. 'So you'll stay around the region.'

'Maybe. I might go abroad.'

His eyes narrowed sharply. 'Abroad?'

'It was just an idea—I've only just had it,' she said, and wondered why she hadn't thought of it before. She could get right away, forget about him, please herself. That was one of the joys of being single, you could be utterly selfish.

And it was a hollow and empty way to fill your life, she acknowledged. She smiled brightly. 'Right, I'd better go and freshen up ready for the day. I'll see you down here later,' she said, and, pushing back her chair, she headed out of the dining room, unaware of the thoughtful look on his face.

'So, that's it.'

Kate's eyes met Oliver's briefly and skittered away.

'Yes. It was a good conference. Lots of useful material.'

'Will I see you again?'

She hesitated, but before she could speak, his mobile phone rang. With a muttered oath he pulled it out of his pocket and glanced at it, all ready to switch it off without answering, but it was his brother's home number—and Steve was abroad.

'Julia,' he said, watching Kate to make sure she didn't slip off while he was otherwise occupied, but after his sister-in-law's first few words a chill ran over him and he forgot all about Kate's presence.

'What do you mean, you aren't feeling right? Tell me exactly what's wrong.'

'I've got a headache,' she said, sounding weary and tearful. 'My eyes are blurry, and I've got stomach-ache—I don't know, I feel dreadful, and my face is all fat.'

Almost certain of the diagnosis even from that, he asked, 'What was your blood pressure like at your last antenatal?' And then groaned inwardly at her reply.

'I don't know. I missed it—one of the children was sick.'

His peripheral vision picked up Kate, hesitating in the act of checking out and coming over to him, her face concerned.

'How's your urine output?' he asked Julia.

'Urine?' she repeated, sounding surprised. 'Um—I don't know. Less, maybe? Why?'

'And has your weight gone up at all?'

'I don't know. I weighed myself on Tuesday, I think. Do you want me to check?'

'Yes, please. I'll hold on while you do it.'

He put his hand over the phone and looked at Kate.

'Pre-eclampsia?' she murmured, and he shrugged and nodded.

'Sounds possible. And Steve's in Germany—Julia? I'm sorry, I didn't catch that.'

'I've gone up two kilos. That's a lot. Oliver, what's wrong with me?'

He closed his eyes briefly and dragged a hand over his face. 'OK. I think you might have a condition called pre-eclampsia. You'll be all right, but it does need urgent treatment. Have you contacted your midwife?'

'I can't get her—and the surgery's closed and the on-call doctor can't get to me for two hours, but I feel so ill, Oliver, and I don't know what to do.'

'I'll come, don't worry. You'll be all right. Now, here's what I want you to do. Go and lie down on the sofa on your left-hand side, call your neighbour and ask her to come round, and shut the children in with you so you can watch them from the sofa until she gets there. And then call an ambulance, and tell them you've spoken to me and you might have pre-eclampsia. If they come before I arrive, go with them, leave the children with your neighbour and I'll look after them. If she can't help, take them with you and I'll see you at the hospital.'

'Do I have to go to the hospital?'

'Yes,' he said firmly. 'You have to. And, Julia?'

'Yes?' She sounded terrified.

'Don't worry. You'll be all right, I promise.'

'Steve—'

'I'll contact Steve. You just lie down and ring for help, OK?'

He reassured her once more, shut the phone and tipped his head back, staring blindly at the ceiling. He had to go to her, but if Steve couldn't get home tonight, he'd have to stay and look after the kids. His

mother couldn't manage them alone, and they were
one down at the surgery as it was.

'Is there anything I can do?'

He looked down at Kate blankly for a moment,
then inspiration came.

'Do you really mean that, or is it an empty gesture?
Steve's in Germany, someone needs to look after the
four children and my mother's just not up to it any
more, and I've got two surgeries and an antenatal
clinic tomorrow. Could you bail me out until Steve
gets back? You said you're still registered in this
health authority—could you take over from me for a
day or two as a locum? I'll clear it with Peter.'

Bless her heart, Kate didn't even hesitate.

'Of course I'll do it,' she said. 'You go.'

'You'll need my house and surgery keys,' he said,
pulling the bunch out of his pocket and taking the car
keys off the ring. 'Give me your mobile number, I'll
put it in my phone.' He keyed it in, then slipped his
phone in his pocket and picked up his case. 'My mobile number's on the notice-board in the kitchen, next
to the phone. Ring me if you need anything.'

'Where do you live?' she asked, and he could have
kicked himself. Of course she didn't know, but he
didn't have time to worry about it now. She'd find
out soon enough.

'Go past the surgery, up the hill and turn left at the
top. It's the third house on the right. You'll know it.
I'll ring you.'

He hesitated, then stooped and pressed a quick,
hard kiss on her lips. 'Thanks. You're a star.'

He threw his case in his car, gunned the engine and
shot out of the car park, heading west from Aldeburgh
towards his brother's house. He rang Steve from his

mobile, using the hands-free set as he drove, and then Ambulance Control called and diverted him directly to the hospital.

It was only when he was halfway there that he remembered he hadn't told Kate about the dogs either.

# CHAPTER THREE

KATE hadn't been to Gippingham for five years, and yet she remembered it as if it was home. On a dismal, drizzly December evening, the yellow glow of lights spilling from all the windows made the pavements gleam like gold, and it looked welcoming and solidly reassuring.

She drove up the hill, past the surgery on the left-hand side between the florist and the undertaker, surrounded by the lovely antique shops and the estate agents that made up the bulk of the rest of the trade, and at the top of the hill she turned left.

There had been a cottage there on the right, she remembered, that she and Oliver had always loved. A real country cottage, picture-book pretty with its dormer windows in the wonky tiled roof and a little porch on the front. His house must be near it. She peered through the drizzle, rubbing at her side window to clear it, and then paused, her heart thumping, and checked again.

No, she was right, it was the third house along—their cottage, the one they'd dreamed of owning! No wonder he'd said she'd know it, but she hadn't understood. Well, she did now. He was living in *their* cottage, and the bitter-sweet knowledge brought scalding tears to her eyes.

It should have been theirs. By all rights, it should have been the home where they'd brought up their children, not a lonely bachelor retreat. Had their dream meant so little to him that he could buy the house without her? She could never have done that—unless—no, that was too silly. He wasn't that sentimental.

Was he?

'Oh, damn.' She scrubbed away the tears and turned onto the gravel drive beside the cottage. A light came on as she stepped out of the car, illuminating her way to the front door, but none of the keys fitted.

'Back door,' she muttered, and went round through a high gate and into the back garden. Another light came on, and this time she found a key to fit. The door swung open into a utility area which seemed to be a boot room-cum-lobby, and this led through into another room. She groped for a light switch and, tingling with curiosity and anticipation, she turned it on.

Slowly, her eyes scanning the room, she closed the door behind her and walked into the middle of the slate tiled floor.

It was the kitchen, but it must have been extended at some time to make this big, square room with a U of units running round one end and a solid old pine table and dresser at the other end under the window. A gleaming white Aga stood in pride of place against the far wall, bracketed by duck-egg blue hand-painted units with black granite worktops, and in the centre was an island unit with a heavy butcher's block top in solid beech. The whole effect was stunning, and she felt the knife twist a little more.

Dammit, she'd always wanted a farmhouse-type kitchen with an Aga, and now Oliver had one, and he couldn't even boil an egg!

He wouldn't have chosen it, though. He'd always

said Agas were hideously expensive, costly to run and much too hot in the summer, so it must have been put in by the previous owners, and quite recently, she thought. Oliver had obviously struck lucky, because the cottage had been in quite a state when they'd admired it all those years ago, and it would have been a nightmare to live in it and renovate it while he had been working.

Kate's curiosity thoroughly aroused, she walked through the doorway on the far side and turned on the lights. It was a fair-sized room that stretched across the front of the cottage, with a door in the centre opposite her that must lead to the porch on the front.

Again she was impressed. Soft off-white walls, a tweedy mix earth-coloured carpet and lots of beams gave the room a restful and welcoming feel. At one end was a huge chimney breast, with a wood-burner standing on the hearth under the heavy oak bressumer that spanned the opening, and a pair of two seater sofas were set at right angles to the fire, bracketing it.

They looked inviting, she thought, and pictured Oliver sprawled on one of them, his feet up on the old pine box between them, reading a book or watching the television.

Alone?

He never had answered that question, she realised. Obviously he didn't live with anyone or he would have told her before sending her in here with the keys, but that didn't mean he was a total recluse.

Was there a woman in his life? Someone to do his ironing and make him casseroles and apple pies and keep him warm on the long, cold winter evenings?

She closed her mind to the thought. It was none of her business. She didn't want it to be any of her business. If he had a lover, she should be glad for him, she told herself firmly.

She cast her eyes over the rest of the room, over the wall of overcrowded bookshelves, their contents spilling out in places, and the old leather chair and the desk she remembered from his father's office at the farmhouse.

A grandfather clock was standing against the wall beside her, its heavy, ponderous tick loud in the stillness. Suddenly it whirred and struck four, and she smiled. That, too, had come from the farm and couldn't count any better now than it had then. It showed the right time, though, seven o'clock, and she realised she was hungry.

She went back to the kitchen, meaning to look for some food, and as she went in the door opened and two dogs hurled themselves at her.

Startled, she stepped back and slammed into the wall, and a woman with laughing eyes and wild red hair followed them in and then hesitated, staring at Kate with undisguised curiosity.

'Oh. Hi. Is Oliver here?'

'No.' She pushed the dogs down and straightened up. 'I'm Kate—'

'I know. I recognised you from the photos. I'm Judy—Judy Fox. I live next door. I've had the dogs for the weekend—I was just returning them. I'm sorry I just walked in—I assumed Oliver's car had broken down or something and he'd hired one. I take it he'll be here soon?'

Was this the woman in his life? This bright, exuberant thirty-something woman with the flame-coloured hair and eyes like cornflowers?

'He's been called away—a family emergency.'

'Not his mother?'

'No—his sister-in-law.'

'Julia? What's wrong?'

'You know her?'

'Of course. Is she all right?'

Kate shrugged. 'I don't know—I expect so. I haven't heard from him. I've just come to babysit his surgery until he can get back, because he thought he might have to look after the children.' She looked down at the dogs. 'He didn't mention these two.'

Judy laughed wryly and dropped a couple of scruffy-looking beanbags in front of the Aga. 'I expect he forgot. He tends to. He was supposed to book them into kennels, but he forgot that, too. Hence I had them. Never mind, he's going to do my cat while I'm away over New Year. I'd hang onto the dogs for you, but I'm off tomorrow early to London for the day and I won't be back till late. I hope Julia's all right. I'll give him a ring later.'

She headed for the door, and Kate stared after her in horror. 'But the dogs— I can't...'

'Yeah, you can, they're easy. The black one's called Jet, the other one's Muffin. She's a darling.'

'But what do they eat, and when? And how about walking them? Do they come when they're called?'

Judy laughed again. 'Not really. Not unless it's Oliver calling. Then they come. They're besotted by him. Jet's the worst. Don't let her off the lead unless you've got a few spare hours to catch her. The garden's OK, though. You can let them out there safely.'

'Food?' she asked weakly, steamrollered into defeat.

'A scoop of dry and half a tin of meat each twice a day. They'll tell you when they want it. Jet crashes her bowl around. And don't let them lie to you, they've been fed tonight. I've put all the stuff back in the utility room here, so it should be fairly obvious. Right, must go.'

The door slammed behind her, leaving the two puzzled dogs shut in with a bewildered Kate. They ran through the house, sniffing for Oliver, and then came and stood at the back door, whining pitifully.

'Sorry, girls,' she said thoughtfully, and sat down at the kitchen table. Muffin came over to her, leaning on her leg for comfort, but Jet fretted for a few more minutes before flopping down, collie-like, with her eyes firmly glued to the door. 'Well, he kept you a deep, dark secret,' she murmured, and Jet's ears flicked towards her, then back, trained on the door just in case.

Kate sighed. Oliver had always wanted a dog. A dog, a cottage with roses round the door and a whole bunch of kids. Well, he'd got the dogs and the cottage, probably the roses, too, for all she knew.

That just left the difficult bit.

Oh, hell.

She stood up and the dogs immediately leapt to their feet and ran to the door, just to be on the safe side.

'Sorry, folks, I'm looking for supper,' she told them, and rummaged in the cupboards.

Nothing. Well, nothing obvious to make a meal with. She looked in the fridge, which wasn't much better, and then found the freezer behind another cupboard door.

There was her answer—instant supermarket deli stuff, curries and sweet and sour chicken and beef stroganoff and rice, all portioned up and ready to heat in the microwave. What a shocking waste of a wonderful kitchen, she thought, and heated herself a chicken korma meal for want of anything more appealing.

She prodded it round the plate thoughtfully. Did he really like food like this, or was it because he still couldn't cook? Or maybe his heart wasn't in it. She could understand that. Cooking for one was a soul-destroying thing, and for a change the new ranges of instant meals were wonderful—but every night?

She'd always worried about him and whether he'd cope on his own, but she'd always somehow imagined him with a woman to look after him.

Ridiculous. He didn't need anyone for that. There was no reason at all why he couldn't learn to cook, and it wasn't because he didn't understand the principles of nutrition—

The phone rang, shattering the silence, and she eyed it warily for a moment before picking it up.

'Hello?'

'Kate? It's Oliver.'

Her heart thumped at his voice, but she ignored it. 'How's Julia?'

'OK. They're taking her into Theatre in a while. My mother's come over and collected the kids, and I'm going to stay with Julia until I know everything's OK, then I'll go and relieve Mum. Steve's trying to get a flight, but he wasn't having any luck. I doubt if he'll be here before midday tomorrow at the earliest.'

'Is the baby still alive?' she asked, knowing that Julia would come first and would have to be stabilised before they could operate. If that took too long...

'It's fine so far. Things are looking better. They got her blood pressure down, but she has absolutely no history. It's bizarre. Her blood pressure was sky high, there was protein in her urine, she had epigastric pain and a horrendous headache, so she's been lucky to avoid haemorrhaging, but there was nothing on her notes at all. I'm just glad she got hold of me and didn't start fitting.'

'Has she had any fits at all?'

'No. No, she hasn't, and things are much better now. It's looking good, thank God. Could have been much worse. Um—everything OK your end?'

It's our cottage! she wanted to wail, but she didn't. Instead she stuck to basics. 'Fine. I managed to get in. You don't do much in the way of real food, do you?'

He laughed. 'You guessed. There's stuff in the freezer.'

'I know. I found it. I also met the dogs.'

There was a moment of silence. 'Ah. Yes, I...um...forgot to mention them. Sorry. Did Judy bring them back?'

'She did,' Kate said, gagging herself so she didn't ask the burning questions about Judy that quivered on the tip of her undisciplined tongue. 'They seem to be waiting for you. Well, actually, that's a lie, at the moment they're waiting for my supper, but Jet's ears are keeping an eye on the door, if you know what I mean.'

Oliver chuckled. 'I do. Don't worry about them. They'll be fine. They sleep in the kitchen, by the way.

They'll try and tell you they sleep on the bed with you, but don't believe a word of it. I'll give you a ring if I've got any news. I can't get hold of Peter, I think he must be away. I'll ring him first thing so he knows to expect you.'

'OK. Thanks for updating me. Give Julia my love when she wakes up.'

She cradled the phone and went back to her unappealing supper. The dogs looked much more interested in it than she was, but she didn't want to upset their stomachs and have a crisis in the morning, so she scraped it into the bin and patted them instead.

Crestfallen and disgusted, they flopped down by the door and watched it mournfully.

She knew just how they felt. Even though she'd never seen him here, somehow the house was full of Oliver's personality and seemed empty without him.

She wondered when he'd get back. Not tonight, that was for sure. She supposed she ought to find herself a bed.

'So, what's upstairs, girls?' she asked, and with one last glance at the door they trotted behind her into the sitting room and then ran up the stairs, waiting for her on the landing with lolling tongues and gently waving tails.

The door straight ahead of her was open, and led into a bathroom. Beside it, towards the back of the house, was another open door. She went through it into a room which, she realised, must be over the kitchen. It was a big square room, with a gleaming mahogany bedstead that she recognised from the farm. She and Oliver had spent many blissful nights in it all those years ago, and just looking at it brought a lump to her throat.

It was on the same wall as the door, opposite a window that must have glorious views over the garden and the open countryside beyond, and she could imagine lying there in the morning with a cup of tea and wallowing in all that beauty.

It was obviously Oliver's room, not untidy but lived in. The bed wasn't so much made as tugged straight, and the dogs leapt straight onto it and lay down looking innocent.

'In your dreams,' she said, and, without allowing herself to linger in the room, she crossed the little landing and checked out the other two doors.

The first opened into a small room beside the bathroom, obviously used as a storeroom and glory hole. The other... Well, she thought, standing transfixed in the doorway. That, it seemed, was a storeroom, too. It was packed with furniture and boxes—more things, she guessed, from the farmhouse, brought here following his father's death.

She recognised a chest of drawers, and there was an old mattress sticking out from behind a pile of boxes.

There was, however, no assembled bed, or any hope of finding anywhere to set one up.

Kate turned thoughtfully in the doorway and looked back across the landing at Oliver's room. Apparently it contained the only usable bed in the house, so if she was going to sleep tonight, that would be where she would be doing it.

Oh, well. At least it was warm, being over the kitchen, which was more than could be said for the others. With a shrug of resignation, she went back downstairs and put the kettle on the hob. Oliver wasn't due back tonight, and maybe not even tomorrow if Steve couldn't get back from Germany, so it wasn't going to be a problem in the short term.

And, she reminded herself bluntly, there would be no long term. This was strictly a temporary arrangement.

She made a cup of tea, took it through to the sitting room and realised after only a few minutes why Oliver had the wood-burner there. The kitchen was lovely and warm, but the sitting room, without the benefit of the Aga, was much cooler.

She gave the fire a jaundiced look. No doubt it would be impossible to light, and knowing her luck she'd smoke the house out or set fire to the chimney. However, there was a throw over the back of one of the sofas, and she wrapped it round her shoulders, snuggled down in the corner of the sofa with her cup of tea and the remote control for the TV and channel-hopped for a little while.

Gradually, though, the cold seeped into her bones and the television failed to hold her interest. Even the dogs had abandoned her, preferring the warmth of the kitchen.

Besides, it was after ten and she would need to be up early in the morning to sort out the dogs before making her way to the surgery. She made another cup of tea while the dogs pottered round the garden then, after she'd coaxed them back in with a biscuit, she shut them up in the kitchen and made her way upstairs, her bag bumping against her legs and her tea slopping perilously close to the edge of the mug.

Finally she made it, and after a few minutes she was tucked up in bed, surrounded by the scent of Oliver's aftershave and the more subtle scent of his body, so dear and so familiar.

Don't, she chided herself. She flicked through a
medical journal she'd found on the floor by the bed,
drank her tea and turned out the light, snuggling down
under the covers and shutting her eyes firmly. She
wouldn't think about him, about all the times they'd
made love in this bed in the past.

So many times, and every one of them special. She
could smell the scent of his body, almost feel him
beside her, hear the soft murmur of his voice, feel the
touch of his hand...

Don't think about it. Don't dredge it all up. Just
sleep.

Huh! she thought, but in minutes she felt her limbs
grow heavy and the gentle darkness of sleep crept up
to claim her.

It was a long vigil, but Oliver was content to sit and
wait, his mind going over the weekend in a continu-
ous loop, rerunning it repeatedly.

He couldn't believe Kate had been there, that he'd
seen her again after five years of nagging and bullying
her mother for information. Not that he was any further forward. He'd hardly made a great deal of progress in finding out why she had left him, but a part
of him wondered how much that was to do with the
way he'd seduced her on Friday night.

Because she had said no, repeatedly, and he'd just
persisted, touching her, coaxing her into it—seducing
her. He felt a little flicker of guilt, but not that much.
Not as much as she deserved to feel for leaving him
like that without a proper explanation.

Still, it wasn't the end. He'd get to see her again,
and this time he wouldn't blow it by doing anything

stupid. He'd make her talk to him, and they'd deal with whatever it was, and it would be all right.

How odd to think that Kate was in his house now, asleep in his bed. He ached to be there with her, but first he had to make sure everything was all right here and hand over to his brother.

It was hours before Julia opened her eyes. She looked around vaguely, then registered his face.

'Oliver?' she whispered, her hand groping for his on the sheet.

He took it, wrapping it firmly between both of his. 'It's all right. The baby's fine. You've got a daughter.'

Tears sparkled in her eyes and she squeezed them shut. 'Steve should be here,' she fretted.

'He's on his way. He's in England—I've spoken to him. He'll be here soon.'

Her hand relaxed fractionally in his, and she opened her eyes again and turned towards him. 'The baby—where is she?'

'In Special Care. She's fine, but she's quite tiny, so they're just being cautious. She's breathing on her own and doing really well, though.'

'I ought to feed her.'

'You ought to rest.'

'But they'll give her formula.'

'No. I've told them your views. They're giving her breast milk from the milk bank.'

She rested for a moment, then opened her eyes again. 'Have you seen her?'

'Yes. She's lovely. They'll take you to see her, I expect. Do you want me to tell someone you're awake?'

She nodded. 'I want to hold her.'

'OK.'

He found a member of the nursing staff, and she came in and checked Julia, then hung the chart back on the end of the bed and smiled.

'You're doing really well. Want to go up and see her now?'

But before she could answer the door opened, and Steve strode in, worry etched deep on his face. 'Darling?' he said gruffly, and, sitting carefully on the edge of the bed, he wrapped her tightly in his arms and held her silently.

'I'll come back in a minute,' the nurse said with a smile, and left them.

After an age Steve lifted his head and met Oliver's eyes, his own bright with tears.

'So what's new?'

'You have a daughter.'

He grinned a little off kilter. 'Thank God. She threatened to kill me if it was another boy.'

'Well, you're safe, then. They were just going to take Julia up to see her.'

'Have you seen her?'

Oliver recognised the note of worry in his brother's voice and hurried to reassure him. 'She's fine.'

Steve's shoulders dropped. 'Thank God. How about the others?'

'Mum's with them at your place. We thought it was easier—closer, too.'

Steve nodded. 'I'll go over there in a while. You'd better get to bed—you'll have to work tomorrow, won't you?'

He opened his mouth to explain, but thought better of it. How could he tell them he'd run into Kate and she was at his house now, as they spoke? Too many questions—more than he felt up to answering, and they had a new baby to celebrate.

'Yes, you're right. If you and Mum can manage the kids between you, Julia and the baby seem fine and in extremely capable hands, so I might as well leave you to it. Give the baby a hug for me.'

He patted his brother's shoulder, dropped an affectionate kiss on Julia's cheek and left them to get acquainted with the new arrival. It was—he glanced at his watch and did a mild double-take—nearly four o'clock. He had a half-hour journey home, and he had to be up in three hours.

And Kate was at home in his bed.

'Katie?'

She made a sleepy noise and snuggled closer. He was leaning over her, his mouth just a fraction from hers, and any second now he was going to kiss her...

'Katie, wake up.'

A warm, hard hand wrapped itself around her shoulder and shook her gently, and the soft cocoon of sleep slipped away, taking her dream with it and leaving her wide awake and shockingly aware of him.

'Oliver?'

He chuckled. 'Who else were you expecting?'

'No one—you included,' she said drily, struggling into a sitting position and wishing her nightshirt was a bit more concealing, but he hadn't put the light on, just left the door open so that the landing light spilt across the floor, throwing the bed into shadow. She tugged the quilt up round her chest and scraped her hair out of her eyes, grateful for the gloom. 'So— how are things? Why are you here?'

'Steve managed to get back earlier than he expected. Julia's fine, out of danger, and they've got a lovely little girl. She's beautiful, Kate,' he murmured, his voice wistful. 'So perfect.'

'Any complications?' she asked, not wanting to think about how perfect their little baby was.

'No. She's tiny, but she's strong and she's breathing on her own. They don't expect any real difficulties.' He paused and looked pointedly at the bed. 'At the risk of being accused of setting this up, do you have any objection to sharing the bed with me? Only I have to be up in two and a half hours, and I can't be bothered to fight with the sofa bed downstairs. Anyway, the house is freezing. Why didn't you kick the heating?'

'I didn't know there was anything to kick,' she said flatly. 'I guess you forgot to mention it—along with the dogs and the fact that there's only one bed.'

His grin was rueful and unravelled her completely.

'Sorry. I was a little preoccupied. So—can I share your bed, or do I have to sleep with the dogs in the kitchen?'

She moved across, making room for him beside her and wriggling back down under the quilt. 'No reruns of Friday night, though,' she said firmly, and his mouth twisted into a fleeting smile.

'No reruns,' he agreed. Stripping off his clothes without even bothering to turn his back, he lifted the quilt and slid in beside her, with only the soft jersey boxers to preserve his modesty.

She bit down the little moan of longing and turned away from him, shivering at the cool sheets against her heated skin, and said a firm, 'Goodnight.'

'Sleep tight,' he murmured back, and settled down

altogether too close to her for comfort. She could feel
the warmth coming off his body, and the urge to wriggle backwards and snuggle into him was overwhelm-
ing.

His arm would wrap itself round her waist, and her
hand would come up and rest against it, their bodies
nestled like spoons in a drawer. How many nights had
they slept like that? Three hundred and sixty five
times three and a bit, give or take?

Over a thousand nights. Twelve hundred or so,
probably. More, even, and quite a few of them in this
very bed...

Lulled by the warmth, she fell asleep before she'd
finished working it out, and little by little she inched
back towards him in her sleep, until she ended up
wedged against him, his arm curled protectively
around her, while he stared blindly into the darkness.

Holding her was the sweetest form of torture, and
no doubt he'd cop it in the morning if she woke before he had time to move away from her, but it felt
so good and he was damned if he was going to let
her go...

# CHAPTER FOUR

KATE woke to the ringing of the phone, and an inexplicable sense of loss.

For a moment she lay still, sleep slowly receding like an ebbing tide, sucking away with it the last remnants of her dream.

Oliver was sitting on the far side of the bed, talking on the phone, and she rolled onto her back and studied him unobserved.

'Yes, I'm back. Interesting—yeah, good conference. Had a minor crisis yesterday with Julia, my sister-in-law, but it's all OK now. I've only had a couple of hours' sleep, but I'll be in shortly.'

He was silent for a moment, and she could hear someone talking on the other end. Whatever he said, Oliver wasn't thrilled by it, and he sighed harshly and rammed his hand through his hair.

'Flu? You're kidding. He can't have it, Peter. We're already one down with Anne in Oz. We can't look after nearly nine thousand patients through a flu epidemic with only two of us, that's ridiculous.'

He listened for a moment, then turned his head and studied Kate thoughtfully.

'I might just do that,' he murmured. 'Call you back in five.'

He cradled the phone, his eyes still trained on her face, and she felt that sinking feeling.

'What?' she asked warily.

'He said I was welcome to find a locum if I thought I could.'

'So why are you looking at me?' she asked, mentally girding her loins. 'I only agreed to cover you in an emergency—'

'But this is an emergency. We're really stuck, Kate.'

But you'll be here! she wanted to say. Helping because you weren't here was different! This way I'll see you, and you keep running around half-naked…

'Oh, damn,' she muttered, and threw back the covers, sliding her legs over the side of the bed. 'Today. That's all, to give you time to sort yourselves out and because I think on two hours' sleep you're probably dangerous.'

Kate stood up, remembering too late that her nightshirt was short, slightly transparent and extremely old, and with her head held high and strict instructions to her legs not to run, she walked through the door and shut herself in the bathroom.

It was a lovely bathroom, she noticed absently. The best thing about it was the power shower that stripped away the remains of the sleep and most of her skin, leaving her wide awake and more alive than she'd felt in ages.

She scrubbed herself roughly dry with a big, thick towel she found on the radiator, cleaned her teeth and went back into the bedroom. 'It's all yours,' she said.

He disappeared into the bathroom without a word, and a few moments later she heard a muttered curse and then a stream of invective followed by sudden silence.

'Did you have to use all the hot water?' he yelled, and she smiled guiltily and pulled on her trousers.

'Sorry!'

He muttered something she didn't quite catch, but the more or less intelligible reference to the need for a cold shower wasn't lost on her. How comforting— or was it disconcerting?—to know he'd been as troubled by her presence as she'd been troubled by his.

She pulled on the rest of her clothes and went downstairs, to find the dogs waiting at the back door. She let them out into the frosty morning, the sky only just lightening in the east, and went back inside to put the kettle on.

Oliver was downstairs before it boiled, fully dressed to her relief, and he hardly spared her a glance. 'I have to walk the dogs,' he muttered, and, grabbing their leads off the hook in the utility room where Judy had hung them last night, he opened the back door, whistled once and disappeared.

'Thanks, I'd love a cup of tea,' she said to herself, and made a big pot. If he came back before it was cold, there might be some left for him. If she hadn't drunk it all.

She wrapped her hands round the mug and buried her nose in it, her bottom propped on the rail on the front of the Aga and her legs glowing with warmth. No wonder the dogs lay beside it. Pity she couldn't, instead of having to go to work alongside Oliver all day. Just the thought brought her out in goose-bumps.

Still, if they were only running on three-quarters of their usual complement, hopefully they'd be too busy to see much of each other. She glanced at her watch. It was seven-thirty, still dark outside, and he was out pacing the pavements or trampling over the fields with the dogs.

Crazy. And not really very fair on the dogs either,

because soon he'd leave for work and they'd be here all day alone. She was amazed he'd got them, really. He'd always talked about them as if they were part of the whole family package—the dogs, the children, the happy-ever-after. Maybe he was lonely, and perhaps she should be glad he had the dogs for company, but she just felt sorry for them.

The back door opened and he came in with them, wet and muddy and revoltingly cheerful, and she looked at them in disgust. She'd been feeling sorry for them, but the kitchen floor was awash with muddy footprints, and they didn't look as if they gave a damn. So much for her concern!

Jet picked up her bowl—stainless steel and mercifully indestructible—and crashed it down on the floor at Oliver's feet, then sat wagging up at him, her eyes pleading.

He ruffled the top of her head affectionately. 'I know, it's breakfast-time. My tummy's hungry too.'

He fed them, then washed his hands, throwing Kate a searching look over his shoulder.

'You OK?'

'I'm fine—but I wasn't up all night.'

'I'll live,' he replied to her silent question. 'Is that tea you've got there?'

She poured him a mug and handed it to him, and he wrapped his fingers round it and groaned. 'It's freezing out there—the wind's raw and I forgot my gloves. Fancy some toast?'

She nodded, watching his hands as he massacred the bread and restraining her smile. He'd never been able to cut bread straight, and he was no better now.

He shot her an assessing look under his brows and tutted. 'OK, OK, you could have done it,' he grumbled goodnaturedly, and stuck it between the mesh sides of the Aga toasting gadget and slid it under the hotplate cover.

'Well, at least it won't get stuck down inside the toaster doing it that way,' she teased, and he shrugged.

'Absolutely. Why do you think I fitted an Aga?'

That surprised Kate. She'd been sure he'd inherited it when he'd bought the house, but...

'You fitted it?'

'Well, not me, exactly, but the company I bought it from, yes.'

'You always said they were expensive and useless.'

'Not useless, just expensive. But the dogs were used to one, and so was I, and in the end it seemed like the right thing to do. Anyway, I thought you liked them?'

'I do.' She looked round the kitchen with new eyes. 'So—you did all this? I'd just assumed it was done.'

'No—far from it. The original kitchen was tiny, so I had it extended and the bedroom put on over the top, and it's much better now. I know we walked past enough times and discussed giving it a coat of paint and a little love, but the reality was pretty grim—much too far gone for our coat of paint.'

'It's lovely now,' she said softly, and he smiled.

'Thanks. I'm glad you like it.'

Oliver stopped, and something unspoken seemed to hover in the air. For an endless moment they stood, eyes locked, and then the faint smell of burning broke the spell.

'Oh, hell,' he said. Whipping up the lid, he flipped the toast and sighed. 'I expect we can rescue it.' He put the lid back down, watched it more carefully, and then scraped the black bits off into the sink before handing her a slice.

How many times had they had burnt toast in their marriage? Too many to think about, she decided, reaching for the knife he had stuck in the butter just in front of her.

They buttered and ate it standing side by side at the island unit, and then he brushed off his fingers and checked the time.

'Better go. I need to get you sorted out at the surgery, make sure you've got everything you need. Have you got your bag with you?'

She nodded. 'It's in the car. I take it everywhere, just in case.'

'Right, let's go. We'll take my car—the surgery's so close it's not really worth getting the car out, but I can't come back for it if I have urgent house calls without disturbing the dogs, so it's easier to take it with me, but you won't be doing house calls today.'

Kate collected her bag from the boot of her car, and climbed up into the passenger seat. Up, because, of course, it was a four-wheel-drive off-roader and Gippingham was buried in the heart of the Suffolk countryside. It didn't snow often, but when it did it was easy to get cut off there, and there was always the mud.

As she fastened her seat belt, it occurred to her she knew very little about the practice, so she asked him to fill her in on the way.

'Well, there are four of us—Peter Abraham, who you've met, who's the senior partner, David Hunter, the one with flu, Anne Roach, who's an Australian married to a local farmer and settled over here two years ago, and me.'

He turned, checking over his shoulder before reversing out into the road, and then drove down to the crossroads. 'We've got nine thousand-odd patients, four receptionists, a secretary, two practice nurses and then a health visitor, a midwife and two community nurses based at our premises. It's a busy practice, quite a lot of young people with families in the new developments around the town, but we've outgrown it hugely, which is why we're building a new surgery down the hill. It won't be so close to my house, but it'll be better for the elderly patients who have to struggle up the hill to us and it'll have more parking,' he added, turning into a little alley beside the practice and squeezing the car in a designated slot behind it.

'Right, let's go. The first patients will be here in a few minutes, and I need to get you settled.'

He led her through a side door with a combination lock on it, into a hallway that led into the hub of the practice, the room where the notes were filed and, no doubt, the coffee was drunk and the day's problems aired and argued about.

Peter was already there, and as they entered he raised an eyebrow and got slowly to his feet.

'Peter, I don't know if you remember—' Oliver began, but he was brushed aside.

'Kate! Of course I remember you. My dear girl, how lovely to see you.'

He took her hand and after searching her eyes he drew her forward and hugged her gently, then released her. 'It is good to see you again, Kate.'

She smiled, a little choked by his warm welcome. 'It's good to see you, too.'

'So—what brings you to this neck of the woods?'

She shrugged. 'A conference. I ran into Oliver, and

when Julia developed pre-eclampsia, I said I'd fill in
for him so he could sort them all out. In fact, he got
back early this morning, so he didn't need me to
cover him in the end, but then you phoned and told
him to get a locum if he could.'

'And you volunteered to bail us out? You little
star!'

She laughed, feeling a little guilty. 'Not exactly. I
was somewhat press-ganged, but I really don't mind
just for a day or so.'

'A day? Oh. I was hoping we could talk you into
a little longer—whoever you were. Of course you've
probably got other things planned. I take it you are
registered with the health authority here?'

'I am,' she assured him.

'Well, a day, an hour—it all helps. Oliver, do you
want to sort her out with a room and a list and a heap
of notes? I'm just trying to get hold of David's wife.'

'Of course. I'll give her David's room, shall I?'

Peter nodded, already punching buttons on the
phone, and armed with her medical bag, Kate followed Oliver out of the office and through the reception area and empty waiting room, both too small for
the number of patients that she imagined the expand-
ing practice saw at any one surgery. No wonder they
were planning a move.

'There's the loo, there's the nurses' treatment
room, there's Peter's consulting room, here's mine,
and this one's David's,' Oliver said, whisking her
along a narrow corridor and opening a door near the
end. 'Make yourself at home—I take it you're used
to using a computer?'

'No, I still write on slate,' she muttered, earning

herself an arch look. 'Well, of course I use a computer,' she said crossly.

'Just checking,' he said mildly. 'Your printer should be set up with prescription forms, and it's pretty straightforward. One thing we do have, though—just in case of trouble—is an alarm system. Press "Control" and "P", and it flashes up on all the computers in the practice and we'll come running. We set it up for Anne initially, and we've never used it except by accident, but we'd rather have a few false positives than someone in trouble with a difficult patient and no way of getting help. All you need to do is find an excuse to check something on the computer.'

'My very own panic button,' she said, and smiled. 'Thanks. I hope I won't need it.'

'I hope you won't. I'm just next door, if you need anything yell for help. We're pretty relaxed.'

'Thank you.'

He left her to it, and Kate spent a few minutes checking out the computer software—nothing unfamiliar, thank goodness, after her cocky remarks—and making herself at home in the room.

She was just glancing at her watch when Oliver stuck his head round the door. 'First patient in three minutes. Come and grab a coffee and your notes.'

'Coffee? Already?'

'Absolutely,' he said with a chuckle. 'I never start the day without one. Oh, by the way, we're calling you Dr Kate—saves confusion and potential embarrassment.'

She nodded. Oddly, it hadn't even occurred to her, but of course it was his home town and many people would have known he was married. Although they might not recognise her now, it could be awkward for him if his patients thought they were back together.

'Dr Kate's fine,' she agreed. 'Anything else I should know?'

He shook his head. They walked back through the waiting room, and he smiled broadly at the patients and said a cheerful, 'Morning, all.'

'Morning, Doctor,' they chorused, and Kate felt their curious eyes on her as they went through the door into the office.

'That combination number would be useful,' she said, referring to the security lock on the door they'd just come through.

'One, five, three, and then two and eight together.'

'One of those nice, easy numbers, then,' she said with a wry smile, and he grinned.

'That's the one. Here—coffee, all ready, thanks to Mandy, and your notes, I believe. Press the call button on the desk for your patients, and if they don't turn up, fetch them. Some of the older ones are a bit stubborn and like the personal touch.'

There wasn't a hint of criticism in his tone, rather more indulgence for the set-in-their-ways country folk he'd grown up amongst, and hearing the obvious affection in his voice filled Kate with regret. She missed being part of a team, getting to know the area and the patients as well as her colleagues. Since she and Oliver had separated, she had felt cast adrift, rootless, and it was a horrible feeling.

She grabbed the notes, the coffee and what felt like the last smile left in her and made her way to David's room.

A gulp of coffee, a quick scan through the notes and she pressed the button for her first patient.

* * *

Oliver got through the surgery somehow.

It might have had something to do with the strength of the coffee Mandy brought him at regular intervals, or the adrenaline pouring through his system in response to the occasional snatch of Kate's voice when the door was opened, but somehow he managed to keep sleep at bay for just long enough to finish.

Then he gave up.

'Mandy, I need a kip. How many house calls have I got?'

'Three—and two of them are next to each other, in Venn's Farm Close. The other one's way out in Kempfield—a child with an ear infection.'

'I'll take the Venn's Farm ones. Can you give the other one to Peter and tell him I owe him? Then I'm going home to lie down till three. I'll be back for my antenatal clinic.'

'OK. Oh, your brother called. Everyone's fine, he said, and thank you. The baby's making excellent progress.'

Oliver smiled tiredly. 'Good. I'll ring him later. Look after Kate.'

'I will.'

He grabbed the notes for his two calls and headed out, ignoring the speculative look Mandy was giving him. She was dying to ask about Kate, he could sense it, but she'd bide her time and not quiz him in front of the others.

He got in his car, headed down the hill to the little development at the bottom and made his two calls, both fairly routine and easily dealt with.

The first was an elderly lady with a tummy bug, and he gave her a few sachets of an oral rehydration mixture to rebalance her electrolytes, and the second was a man with flu who just needed reassurance and advice.

Both of them, he realised, could have managed on their own with sufficient confidence, but they both lived alone, like many of the residents in the surrounding bungalows, and a visit from the doctor broke up the day and made them feel as if at least someone cared.

He drove home, feeling more weary than his lack of sleep dictated, and wondered if he would end up like that at the end of his life, lonely and friendless and sad.

Oh, hell.

He turned onto the drive, parked beside Kate's little car and went in, giving the dogs an affectionate pat.

'Hello, girls. Want to go out?'

They looked at the door, looked at him and realised it was just a comfort break rather than a walk, and lay down again by the Aga. 'Suit yourselves,' he said wearily, and went upstairs to his bedroom.

Kate's nightdress was dropped casually on the end of the bed, and the sight of it brought back an image of her this morning, warm and rumpled and scarcely covered by it, and despite his tiredness he felt desire surge through him.

He didn't need this. He sat on the edge of the bed, heeled off his shoes, stripped off his tie and unbuttoned his shirt, removed it and his trousers and fell back onto the mattress, dragging the quilt up.

It smelt of her.

With a groan hauled up from his boots, he turned his face into her pillow and breathed deeply. Damn. He wanted her, but not just for now.

He wanted her for ever, and he had a horrible sinking feeling it wasn't going to happen.

'Kate?'

She looked up at Mandy as she came through the door and smiled.

'Hi. Thanks for the coffee. You're a star. What's next?'

'Well, it should be nothing,' Mandy said slowly, 'but Oliver's gone home to rest, and Peter's out on calls, and I've just had a call from David's wife, Faith. She says she doesn't think he's got flu, and she sounded worried.'

'Is she a worrier?' Kate asked, already picking up her bag.

'No. She's a very practical, sensible woman. She hasn't got any medical training, but she's not stupid, and if she says it isn't flu, I'd be inclined to believe her. Do you think you could take a look at him? They only live just over the hill.'

'Of course. Do I need my car? It's at Oliver's.'

Mandy shook her head. 'No. It'll be as quick to walk. It's up the little lane behind the church—Yew Tree Cottage. It's painted white with green shutters. You can't miss it.'

Kate found it easily, and as she walked up the path the door opened.

'Faith?' she said, and the woman held out her hand.

'Hi. You must be Kate. Mandy rang and told me to expect you. David's furious with me. He says of course it's flu, but he sounds awful.'

'Don't worry, I'll look at him, if only to put your mind at rest. Why don't you think it's flu?'

'He's creaking.'

Kate tipped her head on one side and eyed Faith thoughtfully. 'Creaking?'

'Yeah. Very odd. Round his chest, when he breathes.'

That sounded ominous, Kate thought. 'What about a temperature?'

'Yes—it's about 39°C, and he's breathing very fast.'

Kate nodded. 'I have to say it could well be pneumonia,' she murmured. 'If it is, I'll start him on antibiotics immediately, but he might need to go to hospital.'

Faith nodded. 'I wondered. I've packed a bag.'

'Well done. Right, let's see him.'

She was led upstairs to a bright and cheerful bedroom, where David was lying propped in the bed. Hectic colour burned his cheeks, and even at that range Kate could hear the harsh rasping of his breath and the creaking of his pleural membranes rubbing together as he breathed in and out.

'Hi, I'm Kate, your locum replacement,' she said with a smile, and sat on the bed, reaching for his wrist and taking his pulse while she watched his chest rise and fall rapidly. 'How do you feel?'

'Bloody, but it's only flu. I don't know why Faith's insisting on wasting your time.'

'Let me worry about that. Anyway, you're paying for it, you might as well get value for money. I want to listen to your chest, please. Can you sit forward for me?'

He did, and she ran her stethoscope over his back and listened to the creak of the inflamed membranes. The breath sounds were patchy, missing completely from some areas, and she folded up her stethoscope and put it away, getting out the blood-pressure monitor and sliding the cuff up his arm.

'Well?' he asked on a laboured breath, and she took the cuff off and met his eyes.

'Well, I'm not going to beat about the bush, I think you've got pneumonia. You've got coarse crepitations, pleural rub, a fever, low blood pressure, a respiration rate of forty-two—I'm starting you on antibiotics now, and you're going to hospital just as soon as the ambulance gets here.'

He closed his eyes and leant back against the headboard, all the fight gone out of him.

'Damn,' he said softly, and she realised he'd known in his heart of hearts what was wrong with him.

'What number do I ring for the ambulance?' she asked, and when he told her, she used the bedside phone to call them, filled them in and gave the phone to Faith for directions, then went back to her bag for medication to get his treatment under way.

'Right, amoxycillin and clarithromycin for starters, and they can take it from there,' she told him, and helped him swallow the capsules.

She stayed with them until the ambulance arrived then, with a few last reassuring words to Faith, Kate left her to follow the ambulance to hospital and walked back up the hill. She turned right and let herself into the kitchen of the cottage that should have been hers and Oliver's.

There was no sign of Oliver but the door was unlocked, so she assumed he was upstairs. She made a pot of tea, rummaged in the fridge and cut the mould off some cheese and made cheese on toast, melting it in the top oven of the Aga as his mother had always done.

She was just about to eat it when Oliver came down, dressed in jeans and a jumper and with his hair sticking up on end. He threw her a grin. 'Hi. Thought I heard you.'

'I'm sorry, I didn't mean to disturb you.'

'You didn't. It was the smell of the cheese, it woke me up. Any more where that came from?'

'If you fight the mould for it. There's tea in the pot. I've just sent your partner off to hospital, by the way. David. He's got pneumonia.'

He stopped dead, crouched down in front of the fridge with the door open. 'What? Why didn't they call me?'

'Because Mandy said you'd come home to rest.'

'Is he all right?'

She shook her head. 'No, he's very far from all right, but I'm pretty sure he'll live. I've started him on amoxycillin and clarithromycin, and Faith's gone with him.'

He stood up slowly, the cheese forgotten, and stared at her. 'Hell. Are you sure he'll be all right?'

'As I can be. He's young and looks pretty fit—he's got more chance than a lot of people.'

'But he won't be back in three days or so either.' He sat down opposite her, staring sightlessly out of the window, and then he turned his head and fixed her with those piercing grey eyes.

'We'll need a locum,' he said slowly, and Kate nodded.

She'd already had time to work that one out, and she had her answer down pat.

No.

Only it wasn't that easy. His eyes were curiously intense, and she couldn't look away.

'Stay,' he murmured. 'He'll be off at least two weeks, maybe more. Stay here and cover him, and in that time maybe we can see if there's anything left of our relationship worth rescuing.'

Her heart crashed against her ribs. She was so tempted, but—no, she couldn't. She daren't. She started to shake her head, but Oliver held up his hand, his eyes still locked with hers.

'Please. I haven't got over you, Kate. I've never moved on, because there's always been a glimmer of hope that you'd come back to me. That's why I bought the house—did it the way we'd planned it, pretty much. In case you ever came back.'

Pain shafted through her, robbing her of her breath. She'd wondered about that, but had dismissed it as sentiment, and yet... 'Oliver, I can't.'

'Have you moved on, Kate? Can you look me in the eye and tell me honestly that you don't love me?'

And she couldn't, of course. She looked away, her heart pounding in her chest, longing and misery threatening to overwhelm her.

'No, I can't,' she conceded, struggling for control, 'but that doesn't mean we're right for each other. There will always be things I can't give you.'

Like children, and grandchildren, and happy families...

'I'll take the risk,' he said. 'Just give us time, that's all I'm asking. A couple of weeks, to see if there's anything left worth fighting for, and if not, then I'll let you go.'

It wouldn't change anything, she knew that, and if she had any sense in her at all, any fairness, she'd walk away now—but she couldn't. It would be the last two weeks she'd ever spend with him, and she couldn't turn her back on it. She didn't have the strength.

'Two weeks,' she agreed reluctantly. 'And I won't sleep with you.'

Oliver studied her face in silence for a moment, then nodded. 'OK. I'll use the sofa bed in the sitting room, you can have my room—and we'll take it as it comes.'

And heaven help us both, Kate thought.

# CHAPTER FIVE

SHE must have been crazy.

She'd spent the last five years trying to talk herself out of love with this man, and now here she was, trapped with him for the next two weeks at least, and all she wanted to do was bolt for cover.

Oliver wasn't going to do anything to make it easy for her either, she realised when they returned to the cottage after evening surgery. That lazy charm was there in spades, and the warmth and openness that had drawn her to him were still just as appealing as they'd ever been. The thought of spending even the next few hours with him was enough to send Kate over the brink, but fortunately she had a good excuse to escape.

'I'll need more clothes if I'm going to be here all this time,' she said to him as they cleared up after their reheated ready meal. 'I've only got a few basic things that I took with me for the conference—I didn't anticipate a two-week stopover.'

He grinned. 'I'd offer to lend you something, but I can't see you taking a surgery in one of my suits. You might look quite cute in my boxers, though.'

His eyes were laughing, but there was a heat smouldering away in there that made her wary, and she stifled her reaction to it. She couldn't afford to show him the slightest chink in her armour or he'd be in there trashing her defences.

'I think I might take a quick drive over to my

grandmother's house and just check that everything's all right and pick up some stuff,' she said. 'I need work clothes and something casual, and boots and a decent coat and all sorts of things, and there's no point in going out and buying them. It'll only take me a few hours to do the round trip.'

'I'll come with you,' Oliver suggested, but the thought of being trapped in a car with him for that length of time was too much. With nowhere to go, she might end up in a conversation she couldn't escape, and she couldn't afford to let that happen. He was too good at wheedling things out of her.

'I'll be fine,' she told him. 'I can manage, I'm a big girl now.'

'That doesn't stop you having an accident. The temperature's falling, and the roads are damp. If it ices over, they'll get lethal.'

'I'll be fine,' she repeated. 'And don't wait up. You're tired, and I don't need you fussing over me.'

His mouth tightened. 'I wasn't fussing.'

'Yes, you were. I don't need this, Oliver. You're going to suffocate me.'

'Fine. Suit yourself.'

He walked off, leaving her to it, and hot tears stung her eyes. With a despairing shrug Kate picked up her keys, slipped her arms into her coat and left the house.

Despite his warnings, the roads were clear, and she was there in under an hour and a half. It didn't take very long to check that the heating was set to frost protection and to let her neighbours know she was going to be away another two weeks, and once she'd gathered together her working wardrobe and some jeans and jumpers, she was ready to go.

She threw her wellies into the back of the car as

well, just in case she wanted to go for a walk or had to visit a muddy farm, grabbed her long padded jacket off the hook by the front door and set off on the return journey.

And it was going fine until she turned onto the narrow lane from Kempfield to Gippingham and felt the car start to slide. She steered into it, her heart pounding, and carried on much more cautiously, but then she saw lights coming towards her—much too fast, and then suddenly slewing round, the car spinning past her with inches to spare before coming to rest upside down in the ditch behind her.

For a moment she just sat there, dumbstruck, but then she turned on her hazard flashers and got out of the car—warily, because of the ice—and slipped and slid her way over to the upturned car.

The lights were pointing up at the sky at a crazy angle, and in their beams she could see curling vapour from the exhaust. The engine was still running, she realised, and some remnant of training said she had to turn it off because of the fire hazard.

Kate struggled down into the ditch, glad of the brilliant moonlight that turned the frost-encrusted landscape a ghostly blue. Under normal circumstances she would have paused to admire it, but she didn't even notice. Reaching the bottom of the ditch, she felt the icy crust break under her weight and freezing water flooded her shoes, but there wasn't time to worry about herself.

She scrambled up the opposite bank a little and peered through the window, and as she listened she could hear sobbing coming from the inside of the car.

'Hello? Can you hear me?'

'Help me,' a voice said weakly. It sounded female,

but she wasn't sure, and she couldn't see inside the car.

'Can you turn off the engine? Can you reach?'

'No. I'm stuck.'

So now what do I do? Kate thought, but gravity was on her side. The engine note changed, and for a moment she could hear nothing but a terrible clattering noise, and then there was silence, shocking in its suddenness and broken only by the creak of cooling metal and the harsh sound of the woman's sobs.

'Hello?'

'Help me,' she heard again.

She'd have to go back for her mobile phone—not that she could have used it this close to the car, anyway, because of the risk of spilt fuel. Before she could call for help, though, she needed more information. 'How many of you are there?' she asked briskly, hoping the woman wasn't beyond answering.

'Three—please, help us. My legs are trapped, and I think my husband's dead. I can't see my daughter.' Her voice was beginning to rise in panic, and Kate cut in to bring her back to essentials.

'OK. What's your name?'

'Jill—Jill Prior, and my daughter's Lucy.'

'OK, Jill, I'm Kate. I'm a doctor. Just stay still and try and breathe nice and slowly, and I'll phone for some help. I won't be long. Just hang on. You're doing really well.'

She struggled up out of the ditch, noticing as she did so the smell of fuel. Diesel, thank goodness, and less of a fire hazard than petrol, but not something she'd want to get on her skin or on the skin of the people in the car. It must be leaking into the ditch, she realised, and then remembered her feet were cold and wet.

With water, or diesel? Both, probably.

She called 999, gave them the location as near as she could, and asked for all emergency services. Her next call was to Oliver.

'Kate? What's wrong? Where are you?'

'Just outside Gippingham, on the Kempfield road. About four or five miles away. There's been an accident—can you come? A car's upside down in the ditch—and drive slowly, for heaven's sake. It's like an ice rink—and wear boots. The ditch is filling with diesel.'

'OK. With you in five.'

She shoved the phone in her pocket, grabbed her bag and headed back for the car. Why hadn't she remembered to replace her torch batteries? Idiot, she chided herself, and then paused for a moment to study the upturned car.

The side was distorted and she didn't think there was any way she could get a door open, but she could see a large, shiny rectangle gleaming in the field beyond the ditch. It looked like a windscreen, and if it was, there was a chance she could crawl in through the gap and get to Jill and her family.

Luckily she'd changed into jeans and trainers when she'd picked up her clothes, and without further ado she scrambled up the opposite bank and squirmed under the edge of the bonnet.

'Jill?'

'I'm here,' the woman said unsteadily, her voice edged with panic. 'You've been ages. I thought you'd gone.'

'No. I was just calling for help. They're on their

way. I want to try and get in to you, but I can't really
see and I don't want to hurt you. Where are you?'

'Hanging upside down behind the steering-wheel.
I thought of taking my seat belt off, but my feet seem
to be wedged.'

'Leave it for now. The firemen will get you out in
a minute. Look, I'm going to try and get in, but if I
hurt you, I'm sorry.'

Kate squirmed and wriggled her way through the
gap, then found herself sliding down the roof lining.
She could feel the buckled metal under her hip, and
it gave her feet something to push on. She grabbed a
headrest and stopped her descent, and managed to
wedge herself.

'Right, I'm in,' she said. 'So this should be you,
Jill?' she said, reaching out to a shadow and encoun-
tering something damp and sticky. Hair?

'That's me. I think I've cut my head.'

'I think you have,' Kate said, reaching across to
the other side to see if she could feel Jill's husband.
'Were you driving?'

'Yes. My husband was drinking—we'd been to his
firm's dinner, and I said I'd drive. I can't get him to
answer—I think he's dead...'

Kate found him, but it wasn't reassuring. His
cheekbone was cracked open, and she felt the sharp
edge of the bone against her fingers. His pulse was
weak and thready, but his airway was obstructed because of the angle of his head. If she turned it he
might be able to breathe better, but if he had a neck
injury...

He'll die anyway if you do nothing, she told herself, and at least hanging upside down his head's pro-
viding traction on any spinal injury. She shifted him

slightly in the seat, tipping his head against the side of the car and the head restraint. She heard the gasping rattle of air entering his lungs, and nodded to herself. So far, so good.

There was nothing more she could do, though. He needed help fast, but she didn't have a giving set and at least he had a good blood supply to his brain. She'd just have to hope the ambulance got here soon before all that blood poured out through the cut on his cheek.

'He's alive,' she told Jill. 'He's got a head injury, but I can't do anything more to help him now and the best thing to do is leave him until help arrives. If I try and move him any more, I could just make it worse.'

'What about Lucy?' Jill asked, and Kate turned her head, peering around behind her in the darkness.

'I can't see her. Is she in a baby seat?'

'She's got a booster. We've just picked her up from Mum—she was babysitting her and we were on our way home. I didn't want to leave her there because she's not well, she's got an ear infection. Oh, God, please find her, Kate.'

'I will. I'm in the back now, looking for her.'

'Is Andy going to be all right?'

Kate hesitated. She didn't want to lie, but she didn't want to make Jill's ordeal any worse. 'I hope so. There's nothing more I can do for him without help, Jill. We need the ambulance, but it should be here soon.'

'Oh, God. It's my fault. We were arguing—he was telling me I was going too slowly, so I speeded up, and then I saw your lights and tried to slow down, and now...'

She broke off, sobbing, and Kate continued her

search for the child. Finally her fingers located a soft, warm bundle at the end of the roof, right down by the ditch and in a pool of something that could have been diesel and water.

'I think I've found her.'

'Lucy? Oh, God, Lucy…'

'It's OK, Jill, you keep still, I'll look after her. Lucy? Lucy, are you awake, sweetheart?'

The little body under her fingers trembled, but Kate didn't dare move her in the dark without a proper assessment. She ran her hands over the little form, identifying limbs, finding a hand and gripping it when it clung to hers. It was burning up, presumably because of the ear infection, and the last thing she needed was to be lying in a pool of freezing diesel.

'Where do you hurt, darling?' she asked.

'My leg,' a little trembling voice said, and Kate squeezed the child's hand tighter and reached out her other hand, wrapping it round her shoulders.

'You'll be all right. We'll get you out of here soon.'

'I want Mummy.'

The child tried to wriggle towards her, but Kate didn't want her to move yet. The pain in her leg was good news. It meant her spinal cord was intact, and the fact that she could talk was also good. Kate just didn't want anything to happen to upset the status quo. It was bad enough that she'd had to move the child's father without assistance.

'Jill, she seems fine. She's hurt her leg, but she's talking and she can feel, and as soon as they get here with lights I can get her out. Now, how about you? Are you in pain?'

'My foot,' Jill said, her voice clogged with tears.

'I just want to get out. I can't believe Andy isn't dead.'

Suddenly headlights cut across the interior of the car, lighting it up and showing Andy's head injuries in glorious detail. Jill started to sob, and Kate shifted position to shield Lucy from the sight. When she heard Oliver's voice a moment later, she couldn't have been more relieved.

'Oliver, I'm inside,' she yelled. 'The windscreen's gone. I need help in here.'

She could hear scuffling on the bank, and the odd thump, and then his head appeared in the gap beyond Jill, torch in hand, quickly scanning the scene. She'd never been so glad to see him in her life.

'What have we got?' he asked, glancing briefly at Andy and moving on.

'Oh, Dr Crawford, thank God you're here,' Jill sobbed. 'Help Andy, please. I think he's dying.'

'That's Jill Prior in the driver's seat, she's trapped by her foot, her husband's got head injuries and I'm not happy about his airway, and their three-year-old daughter's here in the back. She's got leg injuries but she's in a pool of water and diesel and I want her out, but I can't see to assess her in the dark.'

'OK. Right, Jill, don't worry, we'll soon have you out. I can see lights coming. I'll pass you my spare torch, Kate—if I slide it down the roof, can you catch it?'

She grabbed it as it came, the beam swinging wildly around and disorientating her for a second, then she settled it firmly in her hand and quickly scanned Lucy.

The little girl had a bump on her head, a graze on her nose and her leg was bruised all down one side, but from the way she was moving Kate thought she was otherwise all right.

'How's she look?' Oliver asked, taking his attention off Andy for a moment, and Kate filled him in.

'I won't move her until the ambulance gets here— I'd rather have a spinal board to lift her out on. She's been flung around a bit.'

'Good idea. Andy's pressure's dropping, so I'm going to try and get a line in. Jill seems to be all right except for the leg, but there's a little tenderness in the epigastrium and across the sternum consistent with seat-belt injuries.'

Spleen, Kate thought. That could account for the epigastric pain. And then Jill dropped a bombshell.

'I'm pregnant,' she said, her voice flat. 'Twelve weeks.'

Kate closed her eyes briefly and counted to five. There wasn't time to count to ten, because the emergency services arrived then and all hell broke loose. Within a few minutes they'd prised open the door beside Jill, freed her foot and removed her from the car, and they were passing a spinal board in for Kate to put Lucy on while they worked on freeing Andy.

Lucy, however, was having none of it, and before Kate could stop her she scrambled up and launched herself through the door. Kate followed hastily, to find the little girl wrapped round Oliver's neck and hanging on tight.

Her bloodstained and battered little leg was hanging against his side, and Kate gave it a closer look and nodded. 'It could do with an X-ray but I don't think it's broken. She can go with Mum.'

'Want Daddy,' she wailed, and Kate wondered how

much she'd seen and understood of what had happened to him.

'They're getting Daddy out of the car still,' Kate said. 'Come with me, I'll take you to Mummy. She's over here.'

She lifted the little girl away from Oliver, freeing him to go back to Andy and help the paramedics, and took her to the back of the ambulance. Jill was lying down, and Kate filled them in quickly with what she knew.

'Right, we'll get her back to the hospital,' the paramedic said, and the doors closed and they were off. Half an hour later Andy was freed, still unconscious and looking critical, but alive at least and that gave him a chance.

How good a chance, Kate didn't know. She didn't want to know. She just wanted to get out of there, wash off the blood and diesel and get warm. She was shivering, she realised, shivering and filthy, and she wanted nothing more than a deep, hot bath and a cup of tea.

'You're shocked. Come here.'

She felt strong, warm arms around her, and she buried her nose in Oliver's bloodstained coat and hung on tight. Make that hot bath, cup of tea and a hug, she thought, and sagged in his arms.

'Bath and bed,' he said, and she let him lead her to his car.

'What about my car?'

'Are you all right to drive?'

'Probably.'

'OK. Go slowly, I'll follow you,' he said, and she crawled back along the lanes, taking twenty minutes to go the two miles to the more major, gritted road that led into Gippingham. Progress then was quicker, but she was shaking all over by the time they arrived at the cottage. She turned off the engine and slumped against the wheel, shock robbing her of all her strength.

'Come on,' he said, and she felt herself half dragged, half carried into the house and up the stairs. He sat her on the edge of the bed and left her for a moment, and she heard the sound of the bath running. Moments later he was back, and without further ado he stripped off her clothes down to her underwear and took her through to the bathroom.

'Don't lock the door,' he ordered, and after making sure she was steady enough to manage he left her.

Crazy, she thought as she lowered herself into the water. Anyone would think she'd had the accident herself.

She closed her eyes, but immediately she saw again the car coming towards her, spinning out of control, flying past her window sideways, and then seconds later the hideous sound of crumpling metal as it spun off the road and hit the ditch.

It could have hit her, she realised. It could so easily have hit her, and she wouldn't have stood a chance.

She sat up abruptly, showering water everywhere. Grabbing the soap and a flannel, she scrubbed herself roughly all over, trying to erase the smell of diesel as well as the memory.

Finally, her skin rubbed almost raw, she got out of the bath, towelled herself briskly dry and went back to the bedroom. Oliver had brought her case upstairs, and she rummaged through it and found clean underwear and jeans and a sweater.

She wasn't ready for bed yet. She didn't know

when she would be, but just for now at least she had no intention of closing her eyes. She pulled on the clothes, snuggled her feet into slipper socks and went downstairs.

Oliver was sitting by the fire, a teatray on the box in front of him, and he stood up as she came down and led her to the sofa. 'Sit here, I've warmed it for you,' he said, pushing her down into the place he'd just vacated, and then, without asking, he poured her a cup of tea, stirred three sugars into it and handed it to her.

'I hate sweet tea,' she grumbled, but she drank it anyway and it did the trick.

'Have a bit of cake.'

'What is this, a midnight feast?' she teased, but it looked lovely so she took the plate from him and ate it. 'It's gorgeous,' she mumbled round a mouthful. 'Who made it?'

'Judy.'

The redhead. Suddenly it tasted like sawdust, and she put it down.

'Tell me about Judy,' she said, wanting to know even though she didn't, if that made sense. She didn't think it did, but not much about her life was making sense at the moment.

'She's my neighbour. She's also my cleaning lady, which is really useful, and if I'm pushed for time she'll walk the dogs. She's in her early thirties, she's divorced with two children and she's got a cat called Murphy—and, no, I'm not sleeping with her. Does that answer your questions?'

Heat brushed her cheeks. It did, but she wasn't sharing that with him. 'She said she recognised me— from the photos.'

He tipped his head towards the far end of the room, and she looked and saw a row of photo frames on the shelves over the desk. Goodness knows how she'd missed them, they were obvious enough.

She recognised the wedding photo—she had a copy of the same one in her handbag—but the others were family photos, of his mother and father, Steve and Julia's wedding, the children, and a studio portrait of her she'd had done when she was twenty-three, just after she'd met him.

Did he have a picture of her in his surgery? And if so, what did his patients make of it? 'What have you told everyone about us?' she asked, needing to know where she stood if someone got curious.

'Nothing much. We're living apart for now. Nothing more. I don't discuss it.'

'But they will.'

'Of course.'

'And calling me Dr Kate will only work for a short while.'

'It won't work at all,' he told her drily. 'They've already worked it out. Every patient I had today commented on the fact that you've come back. I had to explain that you're just working as a locum. I was thinking of posting a notice in the waiting room.'

Oliver's smile was wry and a little sad, and she looked quickly away. She couldn't bear to think that she was responsible for the sadness in his eyes, but if she came back to him, how long would it be before the sadness was back? The regret, the longing for children so great that it ate away at his love and turned him against her?

He'd hate her, and she couldn't bear that either. Better that he should find consolation with the lovely

Judy, and from the little she'd seen she was sure Judy would be good for him. She was warm and friendly and spontaneous, exactly the sort of woman he needed, and she already had children. Add to them a couple of their own children, and his happiness would be complete. They might not have that kind of a relationship now, but that didn't mean it was out of the question.

Kate forced herself to finish the cake, considering as she did how much better his diet would be with a little home cooking rather than pre-packed everything, and told herself that she should maybe spend this two weeks encouraging Oliver to take more interest in his neighbour.

Even if it would tear her apart.

'You look very thoughtful.'

Kate shrugged, staring into the fire and not answering for a moment. 'Just thinking about the crash. I thought the car was going to hit me.'

'Hit you?' He felt the shock of her words right down to his bones. 'You were there? I thought you'd found the car in the ditch?'

'No. It lost control and spun past me—missed me by inches.'

She shuddered, and Oliver shifted closer, drawing her into his arms. Good grief. He might have lost her, now, of all times, just when he'd almost got her back. Because of it, in fact. If he hadn't talked her into staying with him for the next two weeks, she would have gone back to her grandmother's house in Norfolk this evening and wouldn't have been on that road at all.

If she'd been killed, it would have been his fault.

His arms tightened around her, and she nestled closer. 'You're OK,' he murmured, pressing his lips to her hair. It was still slightly damp, and it smelt of shampoo and diesel, reminding him of how close she'd come to disaster.

'Sorry, I got diesel on my hair, I think. Do I still smell?'

'A little. I can live with it.'

'What happened to my clothes?' she asked, lifting her head a fraction.

'They're in the washing machine with your trainers, trying to get the diesel out.'

'And the blood.'

'And the mud.'

She shuddered again, and tucked her head back down against his chest. 'Do you mind if I stay up for a while? I really don't want to go up to bed just yet.'

He couldn't blame her, and he was more than happy to have her with him after such a close shave. 'Sure. Why don't I get the bed out and we can lie down and rest properly?'

'I'm not—'

'I know. Credit me with a little common sense and decency,' he said shortly, cross with himself as much as her because he wanted nothing more than to bury himself in her and assure himself that she was still alive.

Kate nodded, and he stood up and moved the tray back to the kitchen, pulled the pine box out of the way and unfolded the other sofa. He'd already made it up, so all he had to do was get the quilt and pillows out of the box and shake them out.

'Come on,' he said, and, lying down on top of the quilt, he patted the other side of the bed. She crawled forwards onto it and came up beside him, then cuddled down into the crook of his arm, facing the fire.

'I'm sorry, I feel really stupid, but every time I shut my eyes I see the car spinning past.'

'Don't,' he said, and rolling towards her he snuggled her back against his chest, trying not to think about it. 'I phoned the hospital while you were in the bath, by the way. They're all OK. Andy's recovered consciousness, and it looks as though he's not going to have any lasting ill effects. He'll be in for a while, though, while they sort out that facial injury.'

He felt the tension drain out of her. 'And Lucy?'

'Lucy's got a slight leg injury but she's fine, so's Jill, and there doesn't seem to be a problem with her spleen or the pregnancy at the moment. They're keeping them in overnight, but it looks like they're all going to be all right.'

'Thank God.'

She relaxed against him, and within seconds she was asleep, her body growing heavier. He gave her half an hour, then got up and sorted the dogs out, eased off her jeans and removed his own clothes, then slid the quilt out from under her and drew her back into his arms, tucking the quilt back round her shoulders to keep out the draughts.

He'd probably be in trouble, but he didn't care. He needed to hold her, and she needed to be held, and to hell with what she'd have to say about it. He'd deal with that in the morning.

# CHAPTER SIX

'DAVID'S looking better, apparently.'

Kate, seated at the big desk in the office completing her paperwork, looked up at Peter and smiled in relief. 'Good. He looked awful on Monday morning.'

'Well, he's had nearly forty-eight hours of antibiotics, so he should be improving now. Well done, by the way, for admitting him so promptly. A lot of people would have vacillated and tried to treat him at home.'

She laughed and shook her head. 'Not me. He was beyond that, as far as I was concerned, and I'm not that desperate for a permanent job.'

Peter peered at her keenly over the top of his reading glasses. 'You think he was that critical?'

She shrugged. 'He could have been. I'm not sure. Maybe.'

'Faith was very worried, and she's not a worrier,' Mandy said, plonking a cup of coffee down in front of Kate with a smile.

'Have I got time for that?' Kate said, glancing at her watch. 'Don't I have calls?'

'Yes, a couple, but you've got time for a quick drink, I'm sure. The first call's a lady out at Kempfield, in the gatehouse of the Hall. She's fallen off her bike and been sent home from hospital with a broken arm, and she's having trouble coping. I said you'd look in. Her name's Eve Bailey. The other call is to Lucy Prior, a three-year-old with an ear infection.'

'Lucy Prior?' Peter said, lifting his head. 'I saw her on Monday morning—put her on amoxycillin.'

'And I saw her on Monday evening, upside down in a ditch outside Kempfield Hall,' Kate said. 'It was the Priors that were in the accident I told you about. Her mother wasn't badly injured, but her father was pretty rough—nasty facial injury. They were all admitted.'

'Well, Mum and Lucy are apparently home. I don't know about the father.'

'Oh, I can't imagine he'd be out yet. So what did she say was wrong with Lucy?'

'Not responding to treatment, apparently. She keeps crying.'

'I'm not surprised,' Kate said thoughtfully. 'Poor little scrap, it was a terrible ordeal. I'll go and see her—she probably just needs reassurance from her mother that everything's all right, but it might be that's the bug's resistant to the antibiotic, I suppose. Did it sound urgent?'

'No, I don't think so, but she said she couldn't get her here.'

'That figures, having seen the car. Don't worry, I'll be that way anyway. If you could find me the notes...'

Mandy put them in her hand, and Kate smiled, downed another few mouthfuls of coffee and set off.

Kempfield Hall was on the right, just past the straight stretch where she'd been involved in the accident with the Priors on Monday night. Despite the fact that they were all recovering well, she still didn't relish driving down the road again.

Still, she had to do it some time, she reasoned, and

perhaps it was better sooner rather than later, so she could get it all out of her system. She still didn't really understand why she'd overreacted so badly, but even last night she still had the image of that whirling car in her head every time she closed her eyes.

She just hoped going down the lane wouldn't bring it all back to the extent that she ended up like she had on Monday night, back in bed with Oliver.

That had been a silly mistake. She'd woken at three in the morning to find herself snuggled up to him under the covers and, with him behind her and the fire in front, she had been virtually steaming. She hadn't been able to move, though. His arm had been firmly round her waist and one heavy, solid thigh clamped over her hip, anchoring her in place.

She'd just turned the quilt back and lain there, enjoying the familiar weight of his body wedged against her, and later, when he'd rolled over, driven away by the heat, she'd quietly slipped upstairs to his room and spent the last few short hours of the night shivering alone in the chilly sheets and regretting her virtuous impulse.

He hadn't said anything in the morning, though, just brought her a cup of tea at seven on his way to the bathroom. And to give him credit he hadn't tried to take advantage of the situation, either then or since. It was just as well, because she didn't think she'd have the strength of will to stop him, and the closer she got to him the harder it was going to be to leave. It was going to be well nigh impossible as it was.

Kate slowed down as she passed the site of the accident, but apart from a scuff on the bank there was no hint that such a dramatic event had taken place, and on such a mild, sunny day as today it was hard to imagine the road slick with ice.

She shivered, and concentrated her attention on finding her first port of call. It wasn't hard to spot. Kempfield Hall was a tall, Georgian-fronted house at the end of a long drive, visible for miles around. It must have wonderful views, Kate thought as she approached the entrance to the drive.

The gatehouse cottage was just beside it, as she would have expected, and was a delightful little Gothic building, with leaded windows and pretty, decorative brickwork on the gables. Rattling over the cattle grid, she parked outside and walked up to the front door, revelling in the tranquil setting.

Deer were grazing in the park, and chickens were scratching in the grass at the side of the drive. It was utterly peaceful, and she paused for a moment and let the stillness fill her.

Gorgeous. She could have stood there for hours, but she had other calls to make, other patients to see, including little Lucy Prior. Raising a hand, she rapped on the knocker and listened.

'Come in!'

The voice was very faint, so she opened the door and walked in. 'Hello? It's the doctor—where are you, Mrs Bailey?'

'Through here.'

She followed the voice down the little hall and through a door, and found Mrs Bailey trying to struggle out of a chair.

'Don't get up,' Kate said hastily, and went over to her, quickly sitting down beside her on another chair to put herself on the same level. 'I'm Dr Kate—I'm covering for Dr Hunter while he's off sick. I gather you've had an accident and you're having difficulty managing. I can see you're finding it hard to get up.'

'Oh, dreadful,' the woman said, easing back into the chair. 'I'm so glad you're here. I've really hurt my back, and my arm's throbbing, and I've got to make the supper for my husband and daughter in a couple of hours and I just don't know how I'm going to do it.'

'Can't they manage with fish and chips for one night?' Kate suggested, appalled, but Mrs Bailey just laughed.

'Out here? The nearest chip shop is in Gippingham, and anyway, my daughter can't have fish and chips, she's got a weight problem.'

'But one night—'

'I can't get there, anyway, so it's academic,' she said, so Kate tried again.

'OK, well, couldn't your husband cook it, or your daughter, if she's old enough?'

'My daughter?' Mrs Bailey laughed again, a strained, tired laugh without any humour. 'My daughter's fifteen, but she's a bit of a liability in the kitchen.'

'Would she burn everything?'

'Probably. She'd probably set fire to us as well but, no, the reason I can't let her in there is because of the food. She'd just eat everything. I have to lock the larder, or she'd be huge. She's just so greedy. And my husband works hard on the estate—he's the gamekeeper and odd job man. He's not well, and he's usually exhausted by the time he comes in, especially this time of year, with the shooting, and they're much too busy for him to take time off.'

Kate was still thinking about the daughter and her

weight problem. 'Has your daughter seen a dietician?' she asked curiously. 'It seems to be quite a worry for you.'

'Just one of the many. She has behavioural problems. She's...different.'

'Different?'

'I can't explain it, really. She's in mainstream school, but she has help with some of her subjects. Her IQ's a little on the low side of normal, but she's got an amazing memory. You can't win an argument with her about when something happened—if we can't remember, we ask Alison. She's always right. And yet they say there are things she can't retain! Well, I know she can, if she wants to, but most of the time she doesn't want to. She just can't be bothered, and you know what they say about taking a horse to water and making it drink.'

Kate nodded slowly, her professional instincts aroused.

'The food thing—has it always been a problem?'

'Oh, yes—well, after the first year or two. She was hell to feed as a baby, because she was so weak. I had to bottle feed her because she wouldn't suck, but we were in Borneo, and there wasn't the support I would have had here.'

'That must have been hard.'

'It was. Rob worked as a holiday rep and tour guide, but then he got amoebic dysentery and malaria and had to give up, and we came home. I was glad to be back, really, because it was difficult with schooling and everything. That was five years ago, and we moved around for a couple of years before my husband got this job. But the food thing—well, I've always had to take a firm hand in her diet, because she'll just eat anything, and out in Borneo that could be quite dangerous. She doesn't seem to have any brakes, you know? It's like she doesn't realise she's full.'

Alarm bells were ringing loud and clear, but Kate didn't want to jump to conclusions. She decided to sound Mrs Bailey out further while she examined her.

'Did you have a letter for us from the hospital?' she asked, and Mrs Bailey nodded.

'It's somewhere—on the mantelpiece, I expect. I'm not sure.'

Kate stood up and went over to the mantelpiece, and there, propped up against a picture frame, was a small brown envelope with 'Dr Crawford' written on the outside.

As she picked it up, she glanced at the photo and saw a young girl of about ten leaning against Mrs Bailey, outside the front door of the cottage.

'Is that your daughter?' she asked, and the woman nodded.

'Yes. It was taken last summer.'

Kate looked more closely. The girl must have been at least fourteen then, but she didn't look it. Delayed onset of puberty, short stature, poor sucking mechanism—the list was totting up.

She scanned the letter, learning that Mrs Bailey had sustained a simple fracture of the ulna and no findings on X-ray of a spinal fracture, but as she well knew from several of her past patients, spinal problems didn't necessarily show on X-rays and could be debilitating.

Reaching out her hand, Kate gently took hold of Mrs Bailey's fingers and felt them. They were warm and only slightly swollen, and Eve could flex them when asked. No problems with that so far, then, Kate thought, and her back would probably settle with rest and pain relief.

'Well, that seems fine,' she said, releasing her patient's fingers. 'So how did you fall off your bike—was that on the ice? There was another accident just up the road on Monday night.'

She shook her head. 'No. It was yesterday morning, after they took that car out of the ditch. They must have spilt oil on the road or something, because the back wheel just went out from under me and dumped me on the road. It was ages before anyone came along to help me. It was just round the bend, at the beginning of that straight bit.'

Kate nodded. 'I know where you mean. I was there—the car just missed me. I helped them get the family out.'

'Are they all right?' Mrs Bailey asked, her gentle face concerned. 'The car looked a dreadful mess when I passed it earlier.'

'It was. I think they are all right, though. Now, your arm looks quite good, considering, but you've obviously got other bumps and bruises. Where else do you hurt? Your back's obviously giving you a lot of trouble, but they didn't find anything, I gather.'

'Oh, I know, but I've really jarred it, and standing is agony. If you could just give me some pills so I can get in the kitchen and sort out some supper for the family, then I don't have to worry.'

Kate frowned slightly. 'I'll happily give you pills, but I really think you should be in bed, resting, especially if you've got any leg pain. Is there no way your husband can finish early and supervise your daughter and cook something for all of you, just for a couple of nights?'

Eve shook her head. 'He won't be in tonight until eight or so—he's working late up at the hall, trying to finish off some decorating before the new shooting party comes on Saturday, and I can't let Alison in the kitchen on her own.'

Kate sat back thoughtfully. 'Mrs Bailey, has anybody ever suggested that Alison might have something wrong with her?'

'What, apart from being greedy and a bit slow at some subjects at school, and having a shocking temper?' She gave a short huff of laughter and shook her head. 'Everyone's got a suggestion. Some people say she's just a bit slow, others say she's stubborn—someone tried to suggest she'd got Down's, but I know she hasn't. She doesn't look like that, you can see that from the photo, but I know there's something wrong.'

'Were any of these people health or education professionals?'

'Some of them. One teacher was concerned—that was when she started getting a little help in some subjects, but on the whole she's quite bright, really. Dinner ladies at school have been concerned about the food aspect, and my friends, parents of girls she's met through school—they've all had something to say, but most of the time it's not constructive.'

'How tall is she?' Kate asked, thinking of the photo.

'Oh, she's short—under five foot. She hasn't grown or started her periods yet, and she's not showing any signs of developing. It's been worrying me, actually. I mean, I know she hasn't got Down's but I know there's something. Rob says I'm being silly, she must have had a problem at birth, but I really don't think she did. It's like it's more than one problem, but all connected.'

'Has she ever been examined by a doctor to try and find out any more?' Kate asked, wondering just what, if anything, Eve thought was wrong with her daughter. She herself had a sneaking suspicion, but without meeting the girl and getting a chromosome analysis it was impossible to be certain.

Eve was shaking her head. 'No. She's never been ill—and even if she was, she wouldn't take any pills or let you near her with any cream or anything. We've had problems before when she had a stye in her eye, and she wouldn't let me put any ointment on it. She's got it into her head that medicines are poisonous—she heard it once on the television and you can't tell her any different. She's retained that, I can tell you!'

She tipped her head on one side and looked searchingly at Kate. 'You believe me, don't you? You think there's something wrong with her.'

Kate nodded slowly. 'I think it is possible. Without examining her or getting her chromosomes looked at, it's not possible to be sure, but there is a condition, with very distinct and complicated patterns, which like Down's is caused by a defect on one chromosome. Babies tend to be floppy at birth, have trouble feeding, no appetite at first, and then once it switches on, it just doesn't ever switch off.

'They tend to be short, puberty is delayed, sometimes indefinitely, they might have almond-shaped eyes, they tend to have behavioural problems and low IQ—but nothing seems related, and it's very rare, so it can go undiagnosed for years.'

Eve nodded slowly. 'It all makes perfect sense,' she said, her voice a little dazed. 'What's it called?'

'PWS—Prader-Willi syndrome. It's named after the doctors who first described it. I'll see if I can find you any information about it but, as I say, I can't be sure of a diagnosis without tests, so I don't want you getting worried—'

'Worried?' Eve laughed. 'I've been worried for fifteen years. To know there must be a reason, that I'm not just going mad or a bad mother or did something wrong in labour or haven't brought her up properly or stimulated her enough as a child—do you have any idea what it would mean, to know that I was right? That there is something wrong with her? I'm not worried, Doctor. I'm relieved someone's listening at last—but it doesn't help me with tonight.'

'No. Well, it goes against the grain, but I'll give you some strong painkillers to get you through the next few hours, but you must promise me you'll rest as much as possible when you can.'

'I will. I'll be all right once we've had supper. She'll just sit down and do her jigsaw, like she does every evening. That's what I mean about her retaining things and not being stupid. You should see the picture she's working on now—it's so complicated I couldn't do it, but she just gets on with it and she gets furious if I move it or lose a piece.'

She pointed at the table in the corner, and Kate looked at it and saw a huge jigsaw under construction. It was being pieced together carefully and methodically, and it was as if this was something the girl could manage and take pride in.

Kate nodded slowly and thoughtfully. 'Eve, I'll

come back and see you tomorrow, if I may? Who's your regular GP? Is it Dr Crawford?'

'That's who we're registered with, but I've never seen him. Rob has, because he's still got problems from the dysentery, but I've never needed him and nor has Alison.'

'OK. I'll see if I can get him to come with me, and if we could come in the early evening and see Alison—you don't have to say anything to her, but it would be useful to meet her, and I'd like to make sure you're managing all right.'

'Of course—but I won't say anything to Rob, not yet. It'll just worry him. He's managed not to think too much about it until now—I think he feels if he ignores it for long enough, it'll go away, but of course it won't, will it? Not ever, and what will happen to her when we die? She'll never be able to look after herself.'

Her fingers knotted together. Wringing her hands, Kate thought, quite literally—and it wouldn't do her fracture any good.

'One thing at a time,' she said, taking Eve's hands. 'Let's get you better, and get Dr Crawford to give his opinion on whether or not Alison needs tests, and we'll go from there. If it is PWS, there are things that can be done while she's at school, and places she can go later on where her condition will be understood and she can be helped to make the most of her talents. I'll see what I can find out—do you have internet access?'

Eve laughed a little bitterly. 'We don't even have a computer. I got her a little music system for her birthday, and she put it through the window two days later because she said it wasn't working. She just didn't know how to operate it, and it made her angry. It's such a shame. She's like the little girl that had a little curl. When she's good, she's lovely—sweet and affectionate and so kind. When she's bad, she's horrible—and the worst thing is you never know what you're going to get.'

Kate stood up again. 'It must be very difficult. I'll see what I can do to get you some help, whatever's wrong with her. If it is PWS you'll probably be entitled to a support worker to help you cope, and respite care so you and your husband can have a break from time to time. I'll be back tomorrow with Dr Crawford and some more information, but I really have to go now. I've got other calls, and an antenatal clinic this afternoon.'

'I'm sorry,' Eve said heavily. 'I've taken hours of your time.'

'Don't worry. That's what I'm for. Here, some pills to see you through until tomorrow,' she said, handing her patient some paracetamol and codeine tablets. 'Take two now, and two before you go to bed. No more than eight a day, and beware—the codeine might make you a little woozy and it'll bung you up, so eat lots of fruit and veg.'

'I've got no choice, I'm a vegetarian,' she said with a smile. 'Thank you, Doctor. You've been very kind.'

'Don't mention it.'

Kate fetched her a glass of water from the kitchen, and left Eve to it, hurrying on to her next patient, little Lucy Prior.

By the time she got there Jill had settled her down on the sofa for a rest. Kate looked at Lucy quickly and agreed that there was nothing to worry about as far as the ear infection was concerned.

'I expect it's just the aftermath,' she said, and Jill nodded.

'I think so. She seems much better since I rang. I'm sorry to get you out under false pretences, but I was just a bit worried, with the accident and everything...'

'And you? How are you?'

She shrugged. 'Fine. Shocked, I suppose. Grateful that it wasn't worse. Apart from a sore ankle, a tender sternum and a hugely colourful bruise on my forehead, I seem to have got away with it, and the baby seems to have escaped unharmed. They think it's likely, apparently, that Andy and I bumped heads as the car rolled, hence his fractured cheekbone, so he definitely came off worst!'

'How is he?' Kate asked, and was relieved to hear he was doing well. After she'd had to move his head to improve his airway, she'd been very concerned about any possible neck injury, but she'd had no choice, a fact she'd had to keep reminding herself of. Luckily for all of them there'd been no untoward consequences and she'd almost certainly saved his life.

'Well, if you don't need me, I'll get on back. I'm glad you're all OK.'

'I'm sorry to trouble you—you're going to regret taking on this locum job!' Jill said with a smile.

'Nonsense.' It wasn't, in fact, but it was nothing to do with Jill and much more to do with Oliver and how hard it would be to leave.

'Prader-Willi syndrome? Are you sure?'

'Pretty sure—as sure as I can be.'

Kate ran over the conversation she'd had with Eve Bailey, and Oliver nodded slowly.

'Well, you could very well be right. It certainly sounds possible. I think I've got a video at home, actually. We'll have to watch it this evening—oh, blast! I'm supposed to be going to see Julia and the baby. Well, we can watch it later, when we get back.'

'We?' Kate said warily.

He shrugged. 'I thought you might like to come— see them again, meet the new children, say hello to my mother.'

She felt a shiver of dread run over her. Hello, and by the way, we might or might not be picking up our marriage where we left off? 'That'll be a fascinating little conversation!' she said drily. 'I might give it a miss, if you don't mind. I don't see the point of stirring them all up.'

'What? Just on the off-chance, you mean?' he said with a touch of irony.

Oh, lord. Did he know she had no intention of rethinking her position on their marriage? She looked away, wary of those searching grey eyes of his, and shrugged. 'You *know* what I mean. It could be awkward—and, anyway, I don't want to steal Julia's thunder. She'll want to show her new baby off.'

'She's done that. She's had since Monday. Believe me, the baby's been shown off and she's bored to death. She'd love to see you again, she's always said how much she liked you.'

Which was more than his mother had said, she was certain—especially since Kate had walked out on her son.

'Anyway, I've already told them you're here,' he added, dispatching her main argument at a stroke.

She gave a strangled laugh. 'Oh, I should think that

went down like a concrete parachute! Whatever did you say?'

'That we'd bumped into each other at the conference, that you'd offered to help us out at the practice—nothing about us getting back together, but I know they'd all like us to.'

They aren't alone, Kate thought unhappily. Unfortunately, though, it ain't ever gonna happen.

'So—will you come? Julia would be really pleased.'

Kate nodded, a trifle reluctantly. She'd always liked Julia, too, and it would be lovely to see her again and to meet her growing family. Oliver's mother she was less sure about. She was devoted to her family, and Kate was certain she'd find it hard to forgive her daughter-in-law for leaving her beloved younger son.

Oh, well, she'd just have to deal with it. She wasn't the only one who was having a hard time over it, Kate reminded herself.

'You don't seem to have left me a choice,' she said a little shortly, 'but don't abandon me with your mother, please.'

Oliver's smile was slow and understanding, and melted her insides. 'I won't—I promise. It'll be fine.'

If only she could be so sure...

# CHAPTER SEVEN

IT WAS the most sublime form of torture Oliver could have devised.

They arrived to a riotous welcome from the children, and once the shrieks of 'Uncle Oliver!' had died away, there was an awkward silence that hung over the little side ward.

Julia broke it, dear, sweet Julia who'd always been kind to her and made her welcome. With a little cry of delight, she held out her arms and Kate went into them, her eyes filled with tears, and hugged her gently.

'It's really good to see you,' she whispered unsteadily.

'You, too. Let me look at you.' Julia held her at arm's length and tutted. 'You look tired—still gorgeous, but tired. Is he working you too hard?'

Kate shrugged. 'It's a con. I'm just older. And you—you look wonderful. And you've got five children now! Clever you.'

Steve snorted. 'Believe me, it's all too easy,' he said in mock disgust, and she thought, if only. 'How are you, Kate? Good to see you again.'

He bent over and dropped a kiss on her cheek, his hand squeezing her shoulder in support. He was a nice man. Kate wondered what they'd all made of her disappearance from Oliver's life, but now was hardly the time to ask.

'So, where's this new baby?' she asked, dredging

up a bright smile, and then looked up to see Oliver cradling a tiny, tiny bundle in his arms. He was staring down at the baby, his expression rapt, and then he looked up and met Kate's eyes.

Could anything have been more calculated to turn the knife? She struggled to hold onto her smile, knowing she had to do what was expected, not sure how to do it without falling apart.

She stood up on autopilot, went over, held out her arms and took the tiny girl from the man she loved. Looking down, she saw each perfect little feature in minute detail—the dark blue eyes, gazing unblinking up at her, the tiny button nose, quite straight because of the Caesarean delivery, the rosebud mouth, slightly pursed, perfectly designed for suckling.

This was what nature had denied her, she thought, her eyes filling. This soft, warm weight in her arms, the undivided attention of those unblinking eyes, the utter dependence of someone so small reliant on you for their every need.

Five times Julia and Steve had been given this wonderful gift, and yet for her and Oliver there would be nothing.

Well, for her, at least. And he would only be denied if he was with her, so perhaps seeing the baby was a timely reminder to her not to let herself be lulled by his charm. It would be all too easy to drift back into a relationship with him, but she had to be strong, for his sake. Strong enough to let him go.

'She's gorgeous,' she said dutifully, just as the baby made a gloriously bubbly noise in the region of her nappy. 'And she's all yours,' she added with a laugh, handing her to Steve with relief. 'One for Dad, I'd say.'

She turned to the children clustered round Oliver. 'So, who have we got here? Ben, I suppose, and Lorna,' she said, looking at the two oldest. 'I wouldn't have recognised either of you, you'll be glad to know, after five years, but I've never met you two.'

'I'm Sam,' said number three, 'and that's Joe.'

She solemnly said hello, and then turned back to Lorna with a smile. 'So—three brothers. You must have been pleased to have a sister.'

Lorna nodded. 'Brothers are OK sometimes, but I didn't want *another* one!' she said, her little nose wrinkling with disgust.

'We're going to dress her up,' Sam said. 'Like a dolly.'

'No, we're not, she's a baby, not a doll,' Ben said crushingly with all the authority of the oldest. Sam's lip wobbled.

'I *want* to dress her up.'

'I want never gets,' Ben told him. 'Anyway, you can't hold her, you're too small.'

'Come on, you lot, stop that,' Julia said from her bed. 'Who's going to do this puzzle? Uncle Oliver will have finished it before you've started at this rate.'

Kate was aching to get away, to leave the cosy little scene and escape, but just then Oliver's mother came in and stopped in her tracks.

'Kate,' she said, and her face, etched with new lines since the death of her husband, seemed to pale. 'Hello, dear. How are you?'

Kate swallowed hard. Why was this so difficult? Why was she here? She shouldn't have let Oliver talk her into it. 'I'm fine. It's nice to see you again. I was so sorry to hear about your husband.'

Mrs Crawford's control wavered for a moment,

then she dredged up a gracious smile. 'Thank you. At least it was quick—he didn't suffer as he might have done. And we're all moving on. I've got Oliver back near me, and Steve and Julia and the children, and I'm living in a dear little house now midway between them all. It could be much worse.'

She straightened, putting it away with almost visible effort. 'And you—Oliver tells me you're a GP now.'

Kate nodded. 'Yes. I found paediatrics too hard.'

'But you were always so clever.'

'Mum, I think she means it was too hard to bear.'

Not in the way you mean, though, Kate thought, and wondered when they could get away. This polite social chit-chat was getting to her, and any minute now she was going to scream.

As if sensing her discomfort, Oliver abandoned the puzzle to the children and placed a proprietorial hand on her shoulder. 'Time we were off, I think. We've got a case to discuss before tomorrow, and that means digging out a video and watching it so we know what we're looking for.'

'Come back,' Julia said, holding Kate by the hand, and Kate wondered if she'd meant it to be ambiguous or if it had been a simple request to visit her again. But her eyes were meaningful, and Kate knew she realised exactly what she'd said.

'Maybe,' she murmured, and thought the day couldn't get any worse. She was wrong.

Steve, armed with a clean, dry baby, bent over and kissed her cheek. 'You know, you two should try this. It's not a bad game—even when it gets out of control. It would suit you—you looked right holding her.'

The pain nearly took Kate's breath away. 'It's just

as well—I spend a lot of time holding babies in my job,' she said lightly, and turned away. 'Oliver, I'll wait for you outside. Goodbye, Mrs Crawford. It's been good to see you again.'

She fled, leaving Oliver to follow in his own time, and once outside in the car park she sagged against the side of his big four-by-four and dragged in great lungfuls of air.

Why on *earth* had she let him talk her into this? She might have known it would be hell.

She felt the car locks clunk, and Oliver appeared beside her, his face concerned. 'You OK? I'm sorry, it must have been quite tough, meeting them all again. I shouldn't have put you through it.'

If you only knew the half of it, Kate thought, and rolled away from the side of the car, straightening up and forcing herself to meet his eyes. 'It's all right,' she lied. 'I was just feeling a little hot and cold. Must be a bug.'

'Not flu, I hope. Can't afford to lose you.'

'You, or the practice?' she quipped, and opened the car door. 'Come on, let's go back and watch this video on PWS. I'm not convinced I know enough about it to face Eve Bailey tomorrow. What if I'm wrong and I've got her all stirred up about nothing?'

'I don't think you can be,' he said. He slid in beside her and slammed his door, then started the engine and backed out of the parking space. 'We'll see. Tomorrow should bring at least some answers, if not all. We'll just have to bide our time.'

He put the car into drive and headed out of the car park, and Kate leant her head back against the headrest and closed her eyes. All she wanted to do was crawl into a hole, and she was going to have to sit with Oliver and concentrate on a video about a complicated genetic anomaly and make intelligent conversation about it. And yet again they hadn't eaten, or at least not a proper meal.

She had a sudden craving for vegetables, a huge heap of something fresh and green and crunchy, like lightly cooked Brussels sprouts or mangetouts or crinkly Savoy cabbage. The last thing she felt like was a warmed-up plastic tray of homogenised curry.

'How tired are you?'

She rolled her head towards him and opened her eyes. 'Why?'

'Because I'm starving, and I can't take another instant dinner. We're both looking reasonably respectable, and there's a decent Italian restaurant just round the corner. Fancy it?'

'Real food?'

'Not home-cooked, but the next best thing. What do you say? It's quick, it's cheap and it's filling—and it isn't curry.'

She laughed. 'Sounds good to me.'

'Excellent.'


She was subdued, but an unscheduled reunion with his entire family might do that to a person. It did it to him sometimes, and he loved them all to bits.

Oliver eyed Kate thoughtfully. Julia was right—she was looking tired. As if she wasn't sleeping properly.

He nearly laughed out loud. Takes one to know one, he thought. He'd hardly slept since he'd run into her again on Friday. That was—he did a quick calculation—five nights.

He did a mild double-take. Was that all? It seemed like weeks—weeks in which his every waking moment had been tortured by the need to hold her, to touch her, to make love with her.

She was eating now, scooping up tagliatelle on a fork and biting it, the creamy sauce dribbling down her chin and making her laugh. Dear God, she was beautiful, and he wanted her. He was sick of being on his best behaviour, sick of needing her and not being able to say so, walking round her on eggshells when he wanted to yell *I LOVE YOU* at the top of his voice.

She stabbed a spear of broccoli dripping with cream and bit into it, and he all but groaned aloud. Concentrate, man, he told himself, and turned his attention back to his spaghetti. He managed to flick tomato sauce all over the front of his shirt, and when he glanced up she was laughing at him.

He pointed the fork at her threateningly, struggling with his smile. 'Don't even start,' he said.

'Oh, yeah? How are you going to stop me?'

'Don't tempt me,' he murmured, and the tension leapt between them as taut as a steel hawser.

After an endless, breathless moment she looked away, colour brushing her cheeks, and in her confusion she knocked over an empty glass.

Yes!

He could have punched the air in relief. She was just as affected by him as he was by her.

Good. He was done pussyfooting around. There was nothing wrong with their marriage that a little work wouldn't cure, and he was going to prove it to her. He wanted her, and he was going to have her—

and he wasn't going to convince her by being polite and keeping his distance.

Oh, no. From now on, the gloves were definitely off.

The video was interesting, and confirmed what Kate already knew about PWS—that it affected different people differently, that diagnosis wasn't always obvious, and that the earlier the diagnosis was made, preferably in infancy, the better the support and management of the person and family affected.

There were several case histories, but she didn't take any notes. There didn't seem to be any need, since it fitted with what she'd already known. Her early paediatric training hadn't been wasted, she realised, although she'd never met anyone with Prader-Willi syndrome before.

She turned to Oliver, sprawled beside her on the sofa in front of the fire. He was watching the video apparently intently, and yet when she moved her head, he turned towards her.

'OK?'

She nodded. 'I just wondered if you'd ever seen a PWS case.'

'No. It's pretty rare. I think it's one in fifteen thousand or so—that's only something around four thousand in the country, so it's not surprising it hasn't been picked up. I'm surprised you spotted it with so little to go on.'

Kate shrugged. 'It was the key facts—and we don't know yet. I could be barking up the wrong tree totally, and worrying Mrs Bailey for nothing.'

'I don't think so. Tomorrow will tell. Want to look on the Web? There might be something else useful there.'

'Could we?'

Oliver unfolded himself from the sofa and pulled her to her feet, so that she was only a little distance away from him. Awareness leapt between them, and she freed her hand from his and followed him to the desk at the other end of the room.

Heavens, it would have been so easy to step forwards into his arms. Easy, and tempting, but she mustn't allow herself to be tempted.

'You sit, I'll stand,' he said, and then leant over her, tapping the keys of his laptop while she sat trapped between his arms and his chest, unable to move. 'There—right. Well, there are certainly plenty of PWS sites to choose from.'

She forced herself to concentrate, to drag her senses back into line and focus on the screen.

'"Prader-Willi Syndrome Association (UK)"— that looks hopeful.'

They went onto the website, and when it was clear that there would be a great deal to read, Oliver got another chair from the kitchen and sat beside her, so that their shoulders touched and she could feel the warmth of his arm against hers all the way down to the elbow.

He leant forwards to move the cursor, and his thigh brushed hers, hard and lean and radiating more of that vital warmth that seemed to pour off him. She ached to lean against him, to let herself absorb the warmth, to wallow in it, but she didn't dare.

His hand moved to the back of her chair, so that his chest brushed her shoulder, and after he'd shuffled up and down through the pages of the website, his arm had circled her shoulders and she was tucked into his side, wrapped in that wonderful heat.

Kate couldn't move. She didn't dare comment, because she was sure he was totally unaware, but as soon as she drew his attention to it he would do one of two things. Either he would move, which she didn't want, or that incredible heat would engulf them and they'd end up doing something utterly stupid.

She told herself firmly that she didn't want that either, and eased away from him a fraction, pretending interest in the website.

Not that she wasn't interested—she was, and she was sure Eve Bailey would be interested, too, if she could get internet access. She wondered fleetingly how she'd managed with the meal that evening, but then Oliver's body shifted against hers and she couldn't take any more.

'I think we've got all we need,' she said hastily, and ducked out of his arms and stood up, heading for the kitchen. He was right behind her, shutting off the internet connection with a couple of keystrokes and arriving in the kitchen at almost the same moment.

'Cup of tea? Nightcap?'

'Tea,' she said, busying herself with the kettle. 'Don't you need to walk the dogs before they go to bed?'

Oliver knew quite well what she was doing, she decided. He gave a low, wry chuckle and took his coat off the peg, patting his leg for the dogs to follow. They were there, tails waving, eyes bright, and he clipped on their leads and went out, leaving her mercifully alone.

Kate sagged back against the comforting warmth of the Aga and sighed hugely. It was impossible! She must have been mad to imagine she could stay here with him and get away with it! And just how unaware had he really been while he was leaning against her at the computer?

Not at all, she realised in self-disgust. The whole thing had been a set-up, and she'd fallen for it.

Well, she'd get round that one. She made her tea, left Oliver's on the side of the Aga and went upstairs, hoping to be in bed and out of the way before he got in.

No such luck. She came out of the bathroom in her dressing-gown to find him sitting on the edge of her bed, flicking through a magazine.

'Did you want something?' she asked, perhaps a little foolishly, and one brow twitched up a fraction.

'Are you offering?' he murmured, and her heart, still totally his, skittered against her ribs and then jammed in her throat, totally blocking her air supply.

'Still in cloud-cuckoo-land?' she returned, and he chuckled and stood up.

'You can't blame a man for trying. I was waiting for the bathroom. I take it you're off to bed.'

She nodded. 'It's been a long day, and we've got to work tomorrow.'

'And you haven't been sleeping well.'

She cocked her head on one side. 'What makes you say that?'

His blunt, gentle finger traced the shadow under one eye. 'This—and the look in your eyes, and the quiet sighs when you think I'm not listening.'

He turned his hand, his knuckles grazing her cheek, trailing down her throat. He rested the backs of his fingers against the pulse point, feeling the hammering of her heart, and then with a quiet groan he drew her into his arms and lowered his lips to hers.

His mouth was firm—gentle but needy, coaxing

her, luring her into madness. She almost fell for it. She was there, hovering on the brink, unbearably tempted, and then Steve's voice echoed in her ears.

*You know, you two should try this. You looked good holding her.*

Kate didn't know about herself, but Oliver had certainly looked good. The expression on his face had cut straight to her heart, and for that reason she had to end this now, before it began.

She eased away, turning her head so that her lips broke the sweet, drugging contact, and distanced herself from him.

'No,' she whispered, then repeated it more firmly. 'No, Oliver. It won't work. I said I wouldn't sleep with you, and I won't. Now, please, let me get to bed. I'm tired, as you pointed out, and I'd like to go to sleep.'

His hands fell away from her shoulders, and he stepped back. For a moment he said nothing, then with a ragged sigh he turned away and walked out of the door, closing it softly behind him.

She hadn't felt so alone in years.

'Let's find out if I'm right and not just stressing them out for nothing,' Kate said to him, and he shot her a reassuring smile before getting out of the car.

'Just bringing the problems out into the open and going through them with Mrs Bailey will have helped her,' he reminded her. 'I imagine that if you have a child who seems to be greedy to the point of obesity and given to hideous temper tantrums and stubbornness, it must be a huge relief to know that there's definitely something recognisable wrong and that you aren't just a lousy parent who's lost control.'

'She said something like that,' Kate agreed. 'OK. Let's go.'

They walked side by side up the path, and before they reached the door it was opened by a chubby, fair-haired girl who looked about ten.

'Alison?' Kate said with a smile. 'I recognised you from the photo. I'm Dr Kate, and this is Dr Crawford.'

'Mum said you were coming because she's hurt herself. She's in the sitting room. She can't get up.'

'That's OK. We'll go to her. Thank you.'

Oliver followed, taking the opportunity to observe the girl, and by the time they reached the sitting room he was having severe doubts. She seemed bright, able to communicate well, and only the short stature and obesity indicated that there might be something wrong. That and the fact that he knew she was fifteen and looked only two thirds of that.

Eve Bailey, one the other hand, looked older than the thirty-eight years he knew her to be. She was a slim woman who looked bone weary. That could have been the evident pain she was suffering, or a result of her daughter's behaviour. He crossed the room, hunkered down on his heels and took her hand.

'Hi. I'm Oliver Crawford—I don't believe we've met. I gather you came off your bike.'

Eve nodded. 'I did. I'm better, though. The pills are wonderful.'

'Your hand looks good,' he said, examining it while he had hold of it. 'How's the arm feeling?'

'A bit throbby, but not too bad. My back's worse, but then it's not in plaster. It's easier if I move around, I've discovered, so I'll go and make us some

tea while you chat to Alison. She's finished her home-
work, and she's been doing her jigsaw again.'

'It's coming on. I saw it yesterday,' Kate said,
smiling at her. 'It looks incredibly complicated.'

'It is. I like them. I hate easy ones.'

Oliver looked over Alison's shoulder and did a
mild double-take. 'Wow—that is complicated. The
road's all the same.'

'No. It's darker here, and this bit looks rougher.'

She was right. There were differences, but you'd
have to be a real pedant to notice them, he thought.
He was aware of Kate following Eve into the kitchen,
leaving him alone to chat to Alison for a moment. He
watched her select a piece and put it into exactly the
right spot, then select another. She was working on a
brick wall now, each brick just like the last.

'I had a hard jigsaw once,' Oliver said thoughtfully.
'It was double sided. It was a real killer. It was a
picture of baked beans.'

'I've done that one,' Alison said matter-of-factly.
'It was difficult.'

'Did you manage it?'

She nodded.

'One up on me, then,' he said with a smile. 'I
chucked mine out.'

She laughed gleefully. 'I'm better than you.'

'I'm sure. I wouldn't pretend to be an expert on
jigsaws. Do you like maths?'

She wrinkled her nose a little. 'Not really. It's hard.
I like English—and history. I'm good at history and
geography—you can test me.'

'Well, now,' he said, thinking. 'Where's Pisa?'

'Italy. I want to go there. They have pizza and spaghetti and meatballs. Mum cooks meatballs. We have

them for tea, and sometimes we have spaghetti Bolognese.'

'I had that last night, and slopped it up my shirt,' he confessed, meanwhile filing their conversation. Talking about food was a typical Prader-Willi trait, but she seemed so bright...

'Alison, can you move the light, please, so Dr Kate can put the tray down?'

Kate was there with the teatray, with Eve on her heels, carrying a plate of biscuits. Rich tea biscuits, he noticed, and only four on the plate.

'Are we having biscuits?' Alison asked instantly.

'One each.'

'I want two.'

'If you have two then you can't have a potato with your dinner. Just one, please.'

She grabbed it from her mother, who took the plate over to the other side of the room with her, out of the way. She eased herself back into the chair and sighed with relief. 'Oh, that's better. Now, you'll have to help yourselves to tea, I can't bend over the tray, I'm afraid. Do either of you take sugar?'

'I want sugar.'

'Alison, you don't have sugar, you know that. You can have a sweetener.'

'I want sugar.'

'No.'

Just like that, they saw her change from a cheerful, co-operative and articulate girl into a raging tyrant.

'*I want it!*' she screamed. Picking up the sugar bowl, she tipped the contents into her jumper, hurled the bowl across the room and ran out, slamming the door behind her and yelling all the way up the stairs.

Oliver and Kate sat there in a slightly stunned silence, and then with a sigh Eve got to her feet and tried to bend down to pick up the pieces. 'Sorry about that,' she began.

'Forget it. It's what we're here to see.' Oliver stood up, helped her back to her chair and gathered up the bits of broken china from the carpet. 'Is that typical— fighting over food and getting angry when she doesn't get her way?' he asked softly, and she nodded.

'Yes. Absolutely. She'll push and push, and then you have to say no, and she flips. It's usually about food, but it can be anything. She shredded up her word-search book the other day because someone at school had done one of the puzzles, and I borrowed a jumper from her last Christmas and she cut up all her clothes because she said I might have borrowed something else in the past. She's very territorial and possessive sometimes, but she can be so generous.'

Oliver nodded slowly. 'Well, I think Kate might be right. I certainly think her delayed puberty, her insatiable appetite and the unstable temper are clear indicators of PWS, and she's blonde with fair skin and blue eyes. All of these things add up, but she's so bright it's easy to see how it could have been missed—and we may be wrong. I think we need tests, and to do that we need blood from all three of you.'

'All three?' she said in puzzlement.

'Yes. Prader-Willi syndrome is a defect of one sort or another on a particular section of chromosome 15, and we need to compare hers to yours and your husband's to see if there's a noticeable difference. It's quite a sophisticated test and it takes a while to come back, but I've got a video you can look at in the meantime to see if the case histories on it ring any bells with you, and if you can get onto the website of the PWSA organisation, it will give you tons more information.'

'And if it is Prader-Willi syndrome?'

'Then there's lots of support you can get. I know she's really quite bright, but there are things she'll find hard, and she can have help with them. Whatever turns out to be wrong with her, I'm sure you're right—there is something, and it's time you were taken seriously. She's a lovely girl, and she and you need help and support to get the best from her and to give her the chance of a happy and secure life.'

'Have you discussed it with your husband yet?' Kate asked gently, but Eve shook her head.

'No. I don't know how to.'

'Would you like us to do it for you?' Oliver suggested. 'It might come better from you, but he'll need to know in order to give the blood sample.'

'I can't just wait until he cuts himself shaving?' she suggested with a wry laugh, and Oliver chuckled and shook his head.

'I'm sorry, no, you can't. I can leave you the video—maybe you can show it to him. It might make it easier.'

She nodded, then looked worriedly from him to Kate. 'What on earth do I tell Alison?' she asked. 'She thinks she's normal. She has no idea—she knows her body's on the drag compared to her school friends, but that's all. She thinks she's fat, she thinks she's better at some things than others, but she has no insight into her behaviour. She just won't understand.'

Oliver felt for her. It was a difficult situation, and Eve needed specialist help.

'Tell her nothing for now. I'll refer you directly to

a paediatrician. They'll assess her, do blood tests and explain all about it. They're experts, and they will have seen it before, and I have to confess I haven't, so I'm working a bit in the dark and so is Kate.'

'Will that take long?'

'It shouldn't be that long. I'll do what I can to fast-track you, but it's important socially as much as medically that she gets a proper diagnosis and appropriate support and treatment as soon as possible. Don't worry, Mrs Bailey. We'll get you some answers. You may not like them, but I don't think you like the questions either, and you've been dealing with them for a long time.'

They left her with the video and plenty to think about, and headed back towards Gippingham.

'Well?' Kate asked as they drove. 'What did you make of her?'

'I think you're right. I didn't at first, when she opened the door. She looks perfectly normal, apart from being short and fat, but plenty of kids are a bit short and fat. It's very deceptive. I guess we'll just have to hand her over to the paediatricians and let them get to the bottom of it, but well done for picking it up.'

'It was only because I didn't see her, because I caught the mother in a weak moment so she was spilling her guts about it. I think she's just kept it all to herself and got on with it for years, all the time knowing there was something wrong. Propinquity. Right place, right time, that's all.'

He smiled at her. 'If you say so. Personally I think it was more to do with good diagnostic skills.'

'Paeds is my area,' she reminded him, and he laughed.

'Don't push it, I'm not going to tell you you're clever too often. Too much praise is bad for you.'

Kate coloured slightly, and he felt his gut tighten. Lord, she was lovely when she blushed. It reminded him of the early days of their relationship, when things had been going well and they couldn't get enough of each other.

Funny. Tonight it seemed a hell of a long time ago, and he still had no real idea of what had gone wrong between them that was so bad she'd felt she had to leave.

The memory still tore him apart—the shock, the numbness, and then the agonising pain when the numbness had worn off and he was just alone. Would it happen again? Because he didn't think he'd survive it a second time.

He'd just have to make sure it didn't. All he had to do now was work out how.

# CHAPTER EIGHT

'CHILDREN are a two-edged sword, aren't they?'

Kate looked at Oliver curiously. 'Meaning?'

He shrugged. 'I saw the Baileys today. Having talked it over after our visit last night, they came in to ask if there's any way they can get the results any sooner, rather than waiting for a paediatrician. I suppose technically they've waited fifteen years, they could wait a couple more months, but I felt for them. They've been through hell, and it isn't over now, and it never will be.'

'Hence the two-edged sword.'

'Exactly. So I arranged the blood tests, and they're going to tell her it's to find out why she's always so hungry, which isn't a lie. They're having theirs done at the same time, and telling her it's so they can find out what the difference is. Again, not a lie.'

Kate nodded. 'It is hard. I feel for them, too, and yet I'm sure if you asked them if they'd have her all over again, they'd say yes.'

'I don't know. I don't know if he would. Men are more simplistic about such things than women.'

Kate looked at him oddly. Of all people, he was the last one she'd say that of. Maybe she'd read him wrong all along. And if so, if he was more pragmatic about the need for a family than she'd imagined, did that mean she'd been wrong to leave him?

Or perhaps he'd changed, mellowed with the passage of time. Did she dare to hope they did, in fact, have a future?

'What is it?'

She met his eyes across the table in the office and groped for something harmless to say.

'Food—the PSW thing reminded me. I was thinking about shopping,' she said hastily. 'I think I might go to the supermarket now—cook us something real tonight.'

He took it at face value—latched onto it, in fact, and grinned at her. 'That,' he said with studied emphasis, 'would be wonderful. I can't tell you how sick I am of little plastic trays of something indistinguishable and rice.'

She laughed. 'You don't need to. Leave it with me. I'm finished now until four, so I'll go shopping, take it home and come back for surgery. See you later.'

Kate went out, heaving a sigh of relief that he hadn't challenged her, and headed for the shops. What had started as a change of subject now seemed like a great excuse for indulging her culinary imagination.

With that in mind she filled the mini-trolley with fresh vegetables—mangetouts, baby carrots, fine green beans, tiny new potatoes—and moved on to consider the basis of the dish.

Fish? Chicken? She didn't fancy red meat, Oliver didn't like fish, and she was sick of chicken.

So go vegetarian, she thought, and turned back to the vegetables. Onions, peppers, courgettes, aubergines, broccoli—she threw them all in the trolley, collected some interesting cheeses to melt into the sauce and headed for the fresh cream.

Pudding.

She chewed her lip. She didn't have time to make

a pavlova—or did she? It was the only thing she could think of, and in the bottom oven of the Aga it would do itself without coming to any harm while she took her evening surgery.

Five seconds in the freezer and it would be cool enough to decorate—and hey presto!

She grabbed free-range eggs, some whipping cream and a horribly extravagant selection pack of fresh fruit to decorate it, and after a few seconds' deliberation, she picked up a bottle of wine and made for the checkout.

'So, what is it?' Oliver asked hopefully. 'A roast? A casserole? Steak?' He'd appeared at her elbow as soon as she was back in the surgery, inadvertently listing all the things she'd rejected.

Trust a man, she thought, groaning inwardly. 'It's a surprise,' she said, and wondered if she should grab a steak at the butcher's on the way home. No. No time, and anyway, a night without meat wouldn't hurt him. He could manage, and she had an evening surgery to concentrate on.

To her surprise, one of her patients was Faith Hunter. The doctor's wife was looking tired and harassed, and Kate wondered how she was coping, holding the home together, looking after two young children and visiting her husband in hospital.

'Hi, Faith, come in,' she said, rising to greet her. 'How's David?'

'Oh, he's making progress. They're talking about sending him home early next week, thank God, so I don't have to fit in the visiting around all the other thousand and one things I have to do.'

'I'm sure that will be a huge relief,' Kate said with

heartfelt sympathy. 'I'm so glad he's on the mend.' She tipped her head on one side. 'So—what brings you in? I see you're one of Anne's patients. Did you pick me for a reason?'

Faith gave a hollow laugh and nodded. 'Yes. Can we keep this just between us? I really don't want it getting out in case it gets back to David.'

Oh, good grief, she's going to tell me something awful—she's having another man's child or something, Kate thought in dread, but somehow Faith didn't seem that type of woman.

'It won't go anywhere,' Kate assured her. 'What's troubling you, Faith?'

'Well, I would have asked David, only I don't want to worry him while he's this ill, but...I've got this lump.'

Kate's heart sank. Not another man's child, but a lump—in her breast, perhaps? Oh, no, she thought. Not this young woman.

'Where is it?' she asked calmly, and was relieved when Faith turned away and lifted up her hair.

'Here—on the back of my neck. My hairdresser noticed it the other day, and I was just so scared. I didn't say anything to David because he was already going down with the flu, as we thought—and then once he was admitted to hospital with pneumonia it didn't seem important enough, but I've been worried sick all week. I mean, I'm not a worrier, but this just seemed so odd.'

'Let me see,' Kate said, leaning closer and peering at the smooth, pale column of Faith's neck. 'Tip your head forwards for me?'

There on the back of her neck, just to the left of the central line, was a firm, well-defined lump inside the muscle. Kate felt it thoroughly, and it seemed firmly attached to the muscle and almost part of it.

'Does it hurt if I squeeze it?' Kate asked, pressing gently, but Faith shook her head.

'No. It doesn't hurt at all. It's just…there, scaring me to death.'

'Well, I don't think you need to be scared,' Kate replied with a smile of relief. 'I think it's a totally benign growth called a desmoid tumour—an overgrowth of scar tissue probably, from an old injury. They usually occur in the abdominal wall of women who've had children, probably due to the overstretching or bruising of the muscle tissues during pregnancy, but they can occur anywhere there's been an injury. Can you think of an occasion when you might have hurt your neck muscles?'

Faith shook her head slowly. 'No—well, not for ages. A year or so ago, perhaps.'

'And do you know that this lump is new? I mean, is it possible it's been there for some time without you being aware of it? You can't really feel or see it unless you squash the muscle, and with your long hair…'

Kate's question met with a blank stare. 'I have no idea. I imagined it was new, because I've never noticed it before, but I did fall over last year when I was carrying the baby. I hit the back of my head and my neck was very bruised, but we were so worried about the baby we didn't pay much attention once we knew I wasn't brain-damaged or paralysed! Do you think that might have caused it?'

'Probably,' Kate said. 'It might easily have been enough. One thing I do know, however, is that you don't need to worry. You haven't got cancer, Faith. It's just a bump.'

Her shoulders slumped with relief. 'Thank God. You are sure?'

'Absolutely. If you like, I'll biopsy it, but I'm sure it's unnecessary. A rhabdomyosarcoma is extremely rare, and they usually occur in infancy and old age, and in adults they affect the muscles of the arm or leg, typically. With the history of the injury, a desmoid tumour is by far the most likely. However, just to set your mind at rest, I'll measure it, and you can come back again in a couple of weeks and I'll measure it again.'

'Will you still be here?'

That stopped Kate in her tracks. She realised that, without thinking, she'd slipped in to the role of local GP and family doctor, and that it was highly unlikely she'd still be here in two weeks.

Anne would be back from Australia just after Christmas, now only ten days away, and David wouldn't be off sick indefinitely.

'I may be,' she said, 'but I'll leave the measurements in your notes in any case—or with you, and you can get David to check it. It really is nothing to worry about, Faith. I'm absolutely confident, but you're more than welcome to get one of the others to look at it if you'd like.'

Faith's eyes locked with hers for a few long seconds, then she smiled. 'That won't be necessary. I believe you. I'd like you to measure it anyway, and if I feel it's grown the measurements will be here, but you were right about David, so I'll trust you on this.'

Kate could have hugged her. Instead, she measured the lump in the muscle, noted the size carefully in

Faith's notes and sent her on her way, relief putting a spring in her patient's step and a smile on her face that took years off her.

Kate wished she could do that for everybody, but unfortunately there was nothing she or anyone else could say to the Baileys that would sort out their problems, although they could be helped to deal with them.

And, she realised with regret, she wouldn't be here to help the family deal with whatever diagnosis the tests and examinations came up with.

Unless, of course, she stayed. Had Oliver really meant what he'd said about children being a two-edged sword? And if so, did that mean he wouldn't be so worried about not having them as she'd imagined?

But how could she find out? And anyway, it didn't alter the fact that they'd fought almost constantly during their last year together. That could have been hormone imbalance, of course, but on the other hand it might have been straightforward incompatibility.

She shook her head. No. They'd been in love—and they still were. They weren't incompatible, and now her hormone imbalance was sorted out, they were fine.

Except, of course, for the fundamental problem of her ovarian failure. She'd have to find a way to sound out his feelings about that without giving the game away. She'd pretend it was a patient—maybe from one of her earlier locum jobs.

Yes, that would do. One of their fireside chats at night would be a good time, she thought—maybe tonight, after a few glasses of wine and a good meal.

And if I don't get home, the pavlova will be charcoal and the man will have resorted to something instant!

'That was absolutely gorgeous.'

'No steak,' she pointed out.

'I had noticed. I don't mind, I can eat vegetables, Kate, and the sauce was lovely.'

'And the pavlova?'

'Now you're fishing,' he said with a grin, and stood up. 'Come on, let's leave the clearing up for later. I'll do it tomorrow.'

What a fine idea, she thought, and picking up her glass she followed him through to the sitting room. The fire was lit, the dogs came through with them and flopped down in front of it with heavy sighs, and she curled up in the corner of a sofa and wished it could go on like this for ever.

Oliver topped up her wine, then settled back in the far corner of the sofa with one knee bent and his foot up on the cushion, the other leg sprawled out and propped on the box. He looked utterly relaxed and very, very sexy.

No. She wasn't supposed to be thinking about that, she reminded herself, but it was hard when he was so close, his body radiating that lazy masculine grace and energy that fired her.

He tipped his head on one side and quirked a brow. 'What is it?'

Kate shook her head. 'Nothing. I was miles away—thinking about a patient.'

'I'm flattered,' he said drily, and she felt guilty for lying to him. Still, maybe she should follow through on it, use it as her chance to sound him out about childlessness.

'I'm sorry. I was just considering the problems the Baileys face, and thinking about another couple I saw a while back in Norfolk. They can't have children, and it's her fault—'

'Fault?'

She shrugged. 'You know what I mean. It's because of her problem.'

'Same thing. If one of a couple has a problem with fertility, they both have a problem with it.'

Well, that was true, she thought unhappily. 'Whatever. He was devastated, and he refused to talk about adoption. When she raised the subject, all he could talk about was divorce. It was so sad.'

'It happens,' he said quietly. 'We can't cure everything, Kate.'

'I know.' She swirled her wine, choosing her words carefully. 'I wonder what it's like, though, to be going along, expecting all the things we all expect, and be told your partner can't give you children.'

Oliver shrugged. 'I suppose it depends how much you want children in the first place, and why.'

She turned towards him, watching him closely. 'How would you feel?'

'Me?' He gave a hollow laugh. 'Just at the moment it seems I don't have a wife, so it's a trifle irrelevant.' He drained his glass and set it down, then turned back to her, his eyes searching hers intently. 'This business of finding out if we've got a relationship left—it doesn't seem to be making much progress,' he said quietly. 'We're just working side by side, talking about patients, the surgery, other people's problems— anything but us, our own problems.'

That's all you know, Kate thought sadly. We *were* talking about us.

'We know we can work together, we've done it. We know we can live together as housemates, because we're both fairly well trained and civilised. But since you've been here we haven't once touched on emotion, on the things that make a marriage tick.'

'That's not true...' she began, but then thought about it. What had they discussed? When had they laughed, and hugged, and played, and made love?

She felt a tide of longing sweep over her body.

'I need you, Kate,' he said, his voice low. 'I need you, and I'm not getting near you. I know you said you wouldn't sleep with me, but it's getting in the way. We can't be spontaneously affectionate, we can't fool around, because it's always there, in the way.'

'There's more to our relationship than sex,' she said desperately, struggling against the drugging lure of his voice.

'Of course there is! But after five years without sex—and I don't count this time last week, because that was just a knee-jerk reaction—the need to make love to you is beginning to assume fairly astronomical importance.'

Five years? Five years since he'd made love to her—or made love? She met his eyes, searching for the truth and finding it. She felt her body start to shake in reaction. 'If you've managed for five years, another two weeks won't make any difference,' she said weakly, clutching at straws, but in truth she didn't want to be saved. She wanted to drown in the need in his eyes, wanted him to take her in his arms and love her.

'It's different now. You weren't here before. Now you are—and I need you, Kate. I need to hold you, to touch you, to love you—I can't think straight, and I can't sort out anything about our relationship while it's in the way, because I can't see the wood for the trees.' He reached out a hand. 'Come to bed with me, Katie. Let me love you.'

Tears filled Kate's eyes and, unable to help herself, she lifted her trembling hand and placed it in his. 'I hate you,' she whispered softly. 'You know I can't resist you.'

'Don't hate me,' he murmured, and drew her to her feet. 'Just love me.'

I do, she said, but only in her head. She didn't dare let herself say the words aloud. Mutely she followed him up the stairs, her hand held firmly in his, and when they reached the bedroom he closed the door behind them with a quiet click.

It was a clear, brightly moonlit night, and Oliver left the curtains open and drew her wordlessly into his arms. He stared down into her face for an age, then slowly lowered his head and touched her lips with his, so lightly, just sipping, teasing, coaxing her.

There was none of the urgency of their last encounter just a week ago. This was a declaration of love, she realised dimly, a tender dedication of his body to hers, and she felt her eyes fill with tears.

His fingers found her throat, trailing lightly down over the angle of her collarbone, easing the buttons apart on the front of the little cardigan. The edges parted, and his fingers continued their journey, the tips just lightly brushing the soft swell of her breasts above the lace edge of her bra.

His breath teased her hair, his lips moving over her cheek, her jaw, down the vulnerable column of her throat, the warm touch of his mouth sending shivers racing over her skin.

He pushed the cardigan aside, his mouth closing over one nipple, suckling it though the silk and lace, making her moan softly. His arms tightened, and he lifted his head and stared down into her face.

Even in the darkened room she could see the fire in his eyes. Her knees trembled, and he smiled slowly and lifted her into his arms, lowering her down onto the bed where they'd made love so many, many times in the past.

'Stay there,' he murmured, and then slowly, without haste, he removed his clothes and laid them over the chair in the corner. She watched him, revelling in the sleek skin touched silver by the moonlight, moving smoothly over firm muscle and strong, straight bones. His body was beautiful, she thought achingly, lean and healthy, a fit male animal in his prime, and her body yearned to welcome him.

He turned and came towards her, unashamedly aroused, and reaching out a hand he touched her cheek tenderly.

'You're beautiful,' he breathed, and she realised his hand was shaking.

She took it, leading it to her breast, pressing it down against the aching peak. His fingers closed convulsively, then stretched out, his palm rotating slowly, chafing against the lace of her bra. He moved onto the bed, straddling her thighs as he slowly peeled away the cardigan, and then the bra, his eyes never leaving her face.

Her breasts filled his hands, straining up to him, and finally he looked down at them and a deep groan erupted from his chest. His face was taut with need, his body like a bowstring, and she reached up and drew him down into her arms.

Their mouths met and meshed, not coaxing now but urgent, clamouring for something out of reach.

His hand found the button on her trousers, then the zip, opening them and easing them down over her hips, throwing them aside. He levered himself up on one hand and laid a hot, hard palm over the triangle of lace that was all she wore now, and her body bucked under his hand.

His fingers slid under the edge of the lace, tracing the slick heat of her desire, and she felt his fingers tremble. He touched her centre, stroking her once, twice, and she sobbed out loud. He did it again, and she took his hand in hers.

'No,' she pleaded. 'Not without you.'

His eyes closed briefly, and he stripped away the tiny scrap of lace, covering her instead with his hard, hot body. She opened to him, her body quivering on the brink of ecstasy, and slowly, his body shaking with that astonishing control, he entered her.

She sobbed his name aloud, arching up to take him in, and as he moved deeper, she felt the first ripples of release start to spread.

'Oliver?'

'Yes—oh, Katie, yes!'

He drove into her, his awesome control shattering at last, and through the pounding need that arched her body to meet his, she felt him stiffen, his head thrown back, a harsh cry torn from his lips.

Then he collapsed against her, his heart pounding in time with hers, his chest heaving, his head cradled in the hollow of her shoulder. She could feel the tremors running through his body, the little aftershocks that went from her to him, feel the damp sheen of sweat on his skin, cooling in the night air.

'I love you,' he whispered raggedly. 'Oh, God, Katie, I love you.'

She couldn't speak. She just held him tighter, hanging on for dear life. She could feel the tears trail from the corners of her eyes, running down into her hair. I love you, too, she whispered silently. I've always loved you. I will always love you.

His shoulders heaved, and she felt his lips press hard against the side of her neck.

Oh, dear God, she thought. He's crying. A sob rose in her throat, and she tightened her arms around him and held him close to her heart and grieved for the time they'd lost, the love they'd wasted—the love she feared they'd lose again...

# CHAPTER NINE

KATE woke in the morning to the sound of Oliver moving around in the kitchen below. Clearing up, no doubt, after they'd left the kitchen in chaos.

She yawned and stretched, her muscles aching after the unaccustomed exercise, and curling over on her side, she lay staring at the open door and wondering what she'd say to him when he came back up.

Apart from thank you.

She gave a tiny, hollow laugh. She owed him that, at least, for the night that had passed. He'd certainly pulled out all the stops, dragging her emotions from one extreme to the other, making her feel more alive than she'd ever felt in her life.

She'd had no idea her body was capable of such sensation either, even though their love-making had always been wonderful in the past. But not like that—not with the concentrated power of his undivided attention for hour after hour, until she wanted to scream or weep or beg him to end it.

And when he had—then, she'd thought she'd die.

There had been no more words of love, though, and for that she'd been profoundly grateful.

She heard him tell the dogs to stay, then his footsteps on the stairs, and his jeans-clad legs appeared in her line of sight.

'Morning, gorgeous,' he murmured. Setting a tray down on the chest of drawers, he came over and dropped a kiss on the tip of her nose. 'Breakfast in bed.'

She pushed back the quilt, suddenly self-conscious, and grabbed her dressing-gown off the back of the door. 'Back in a tick—I need a pit-stop.'

She fled to the bathroom, to take care of nature and to clean her teeth and stare at herself and wonder how she could feel so different and yet look exactly the same.

Well, not exactly, perhaps. There was a whisker-burn on her top lip, and something different about her eyes that she couldn't identify.

'Come on, slow-coach, the tea's getting cold and your egg will be hard-boiled,' he grumbled good-naturedly.

'I'm coming,' she said, opening the door and walking out into his arms.

He kissed her thoroughly, then eased away from her with a sigh. 'Breakfast,' he said, but there was a promise in his eyes that spoke of a second course.

They spent the weekend playing.

They took the dogs for a long walk, and she discovered only then that they'd been his father's dogs, and his mother had been unable to keep them because of her arthritis and her commitments with her grandchildren. So Oliver had taken them on and done his best to make sure they were exercised and entertained, and they certainly seemed devoted to him.

They went shopping, and lit the wood-burner and toasted crumpets on the top of it, and she lay on the sofa with her head in his lap and watched television while he sifted her hair through his fingers and fed her chocolates.

And at night they made love again, and slept curled like spoons, rising in the morning to walk the dogs again and then go over to his brother's house to visit them all. She ended up with the baby on her lap, but this time, curiously, it didn't hurt as much, and she cuddled her and handed her back when her nappy needed changing, and thought the role of aunt wasn't so bad after all.

Oliver's mother wasn't there, and maybe that was the difference, but Julia didn't try and pressure her and Steve was just accepting of her presence, and so Kate ceased to feel as if she was on trial and just relaxed, and they had a lovely day.

They had to get back for the dogs, and the evening was spent the same way as the previous one, with her lying sprawled across him shamelessly stuffing chocolate and sipping wine and feeling spoilt.

And if that was all life would ever be about, she thought, then they wouldn't have a problem. But it wasn't. Could their relationship survive the terrible blow nature had dealt it? Did she dare to find out?

'Time for bed?' he murmured, flicking the off switch on the remote control, and the smouldering promise in his eyes melted her all over again.

'Time for bed,' she agreed with a smile, and pushed her worries to the back of her mind.

Oliver went round to David's house on Tuesday to see him after his discharge from hospital. He was looking pale and tired, but glad to be home.

'I gather Kate's a great success with the patients,' he said, eyeing Oliver thoughtfully. 'Faith certainly seems to like her, and she's got a good bedside manner, but I guess you'd know all about that.'

Oliver felt his neck heat and shot David a wry smile. 'That is none of your damn business.'

David grinned. 'You're looking good on it—dog-tired, but happy. Is she coming back to you?'

Oliver's smile faded. 'I don't know, to be honest. We haven't really talked about it. It's crazy—you know, most of the time we get on so well, but every now and then I just get the feeling she's keeping something from me, and I have no idea what it is.'

'Ask her.'

He shrugged. 'She's evasive. I don't want to push it. She'll tell me in the end, I guess, if it's important.'

'And if she doesn't?'

'Then it either won't matter, or I'll ask her again. Anyway, enough about us,' he said, changing the subject. 'I'm here to see you. Everything OK?'

'I suppose so,' David said. 'You know the expression "as weak as a kitten"? I never knew what that meant. I haven't been ill in my life apart from the occasional cold, and for that to come out of no-where—well, I was stunned.'

'Kate said you knew it wasn't flu.'

He shrugged. 'I suppose I did. I didn't want to admit it. Actually, I was relieved to go to hospital. I felt so ill at one point that I really thought I might die. Scared the spit out of me. I've got Faith and the kids needing me, and I was going to drop off my perch at the age of thirty from a cold, of all things!'

'Hardly a cold,' Oliver corrected, but David just shrugged.

'You know what I mean. You die of cancer, or liver failure, or a brain haemorrhage—not pneumonia, out of nowhere. It made me think—and I tell you what, Oliver, I won't take life for granted again.'

That gave him food for thought. He carried it with him for the rest of the day, through his patient visits and diabetes clinic and evening surgery, and when he got home Kate was already there, pottering in the kitchen with the dogs gazing up at her hopefully, waiting for her to drop something.

Kate could have died in that car accident, he realised, and the thought made his blood run cold. Each day might be their last. They might not have a future. So many things they took for granted...

'What is it?'

His smile felt crooked. 'Nothing. Come here.'

She went, wet hands held out each side, and he gathered her into his arms and hugged her. 'OK?' he murmured.

'Mmm. You?'

He nodded. 'I saw David.'

'How is he?'

'OK—tired. Thinks you've got a good bedside manner.'

'Did you agree?'

He laughed reluctantly and let her go. 'I told him it was none of his business. Faith gave me a message for you. She said no change.'

She nodded, and he tipped his head on one side. 'Anything I should know about?'

She went back to her carrots in the sink. 'No. Nothing to worry about, though. She came to see me for a chat about something, and I reassured her.'

Oliver nodded. He could go and look in Faith's notes, and if he was worried about her at any time he would do that, but he was sure he could trust Kate's professional judgement.

'So, what's cooking, good-looking?' he asked, his

eyes running over her hungrily and wondering if there
would be time...

'There's a pie in the oven. It'll be ready in ten
minutes. You've just got time for a quick wash and
a glass of wine.'

'Sounds good,' he said, stifling his disappointment.
There was always afterwards. He ran upstairs humming softly, and when he came back down showered
and dressed in jeans and a comfortable old jumper,
Kate was just straining the carrots.

'Perfect timing. Open the wine.'

'Are we celebrating something?' he asked curiously, but she just smiled.

'No. I just thought it would be nice.'

'You want to get me drunk and have your evil way
with me,' he murmured, pressing her up against the
front of the sink, and she laughed and pushed him out
of the way.

'Don't be silly. You'll end up with the carrots on
your head in a minute. Come on, I'm going to dish
up now.'

'Nag, nag, nag,' he said, but in fact it was lovely—
just like old times. He felt a great wave of nostalgia,
and a flicker of dread. What if she went, after all, at
the end of this week?

'David's looking better, but he won't be back to
work for a while,' he said as they ate, his voice carefully conversational. 'I don't suppose you'd consider
staying on a little longer?'

'Staying on as locum? It's Christmas next Monday
anyway,' she reminded him. 'You've got Anne coming back on the twenty eighth, haven't you? And
Christmas and Boxing Day will be covered by the

out-of-hours co-operative anyway, and David might be better by then. Will you really need me?'

Always, Oliver wanted to say, but somehow it didn't seem appropriate. 'I'm sure we can find you something to do.' The pie suddenly seemed curiously flavourless and he put his fork down, all his unanswered questions crowding at him at once.

'What are you doing for Christmas?' he asked, his voice carefully casual.

'Going to my brother's in Yorkshire. My parents are going up the day after tomorrow, and I'm going at the weekend. I'll stay for Monday and Tuesday, and travel back down on the twenty-seventh and stay with my parents for a few days.'

'And will you be coming back here after that?' he asked quietly.

Her eyes met his, then skittered away. 'Maybe. I don't know,' she said, and the dread sat like a lead weight in his throat and nearly choked him.

He pushed his plate away, his meal only half-finished. 'I'm sorry, I'm not really feeling very hungry. There's something I have to do at the surgery—something that needs finishing off. I won't be late.'

He grabbed his coat and his surgery keys, and walked out, ignoring the pleading look in the dogs' eyes. He shut the garden gate behind him, dragging in a great gulp of fresh air and staring blindly down the drive.

Dear God. After everything that had happened over the weekend—all the loving, the fun, the laughter—still she wasn't sure. Hell, what would it take to convince her? He didn't smoke, he didn't drink to excess, he didn't gamble or waste money, he wasn't mean or tight with it, he paid his bills, he helped old ladies across the street, he loved—*loved*—children, and she couldn't complain about his performance in the bedroom, for heaven's sake.

What did he have to *do*?

Oliver walked around for hours, feeling guilty about the dogs who could quite easily have been with him, and finally went back to the cottage, no nearer a conclusion.

Kate was curled up by the fire in the sitting room, fast asleep, Muffin on the floor by the fire and Jet, ever quick to take advantage, curled up beside her. One of her hands lay over the dog's back, and as he came in Jet lifted her head and gave him a reproachful look.

He patted her, rubbed Muffin's head and crouched down, his face inches from Kate's.

'Sweetheart?'

Her lashes fluttered, and she moaned softly and stretched. 'Oh. I must have fallen asleep. Sorry. What time is it?'

'Bedtime,' he said firmly, and put the dogs out for a moment, then locked the door and came back to find she'd already gone up.

She was waiting for him in bed, and reached out her arms to him. He went into them, making love to her silently and perhaps a little desperately. Afterwards he held her close, pressing his lips to her hair.

'I love you, Kate,' he said unevenly. 'Stay with me—please. Don't leave me again.'

But she'd already fallen asleep and his words went unanswered.

The best-laid plans of mice and men, Kate thought on Thursday, staring at the weekend weather forecast in disgust. Snow. Snow over the Pennines, spreading across into Yorkshire by Saturday afternoon and growing heavier through Sunday.

Oh, well, she thought, flicking off the television in disgust and checking her watch. It might never happen. They'd been wrong in the past. She had half an hour before she had to be back for her evening surgery, and she wanted to look in the antique shops on the hill on her way past. She needed something for her brother for Christmas, and a little something for their cottage might be nice.

She thought of buying something for Oliver, but that was too hard. What could she give him—especially if she wasn't coming back?

Although she was almost sure she was. On Tuesday night she'd nearly talked to him, nearly told him about herself, but then she'd chickened out. That was what the wine had been about—to bolster her courage—but then he'd asked if she was staying, and before she could qualify her answer, he'd gone.

Perhaps, if she couldn't get away to Yorkshire for Christmas, she could spend it with him and talk about it. It was time she told him the truth, but she dreaded it. The thought of shattering his dreams—but she was doing that anyway.

Oh, fool, why had she let him talk her into this? She should have stayed away—but what if she was right and he had changed? What if having a family was no longer the important thing to him that it had been?

She wandered aimlessly through the antique shops, not paying very much attention, and arrived back at the surgery with fifteen minutes to go. Oliver and

Peter were there, sitting down at the big table with paperwork scattered about, and they looked up as she went in and smiled.

'Hi. Pull up a coffee and join us. We're just discussing the play area,' Peter said. 'Maybe you've got some ideas. It keeps getting trashed and the toys have a habit of escaping.'

'Maybe because the bad little children play with them?' she suggested mildly, and sat down opposite Oliver.

He was chuckling, and she felt a lump in her throat. His face was so dear to her, every crease and angle familiar, every eyelash with a place in her heart.

'So what do you suggest?' Oliver prompted. 'Ban the bad little children?'

'Sounds a good idea,' Mandy put in, walking through. 'They drive me mad.'

'You and me both,' Oliver said, 'but it's a family practice. We're stuck with them, I'm afraid, and we have to find a way of entertaining them that keeps them out of the hair of the disapproving old ducks that sit in the front row with their walking sticks stuck out to trip the kids up and whingeing if their leg ulcers get bashed by a toy.'

Kate chuckled. 'How about a fence?' she suggested.

'What—electric? Judy's mother's got an electric fence for her chickens. Sounds like a fine idea.'

Good grief. Had he really gone off little children to that extent?

'Kate? Kate, I am joking,' he said clearly and distinctly, and she realised she was staring at him as if he'd grown two heads.

'Sorry. I was miles away. No, I've seen a fence in

a surgery before—a plastic picket fence with a little gate, and they had a Wendy house and all the toys and things behind the barrier. It keeps it all tidied up, gives them something to do and keeps the children away from the leg ulcers.'

'Sounds perfect. Where do we get one?'

She pursed her lips. 'I can't remember where it was—yes, I can. I'll ring the surgery and ask them if they can tell us the supplier's name. I don't suppose it's cheap.'

'Nor is litigation,' Peter said darkly.

'Good grief—you must have had a bad day,' she said with a laugh. 'Right—I'm going to gather up my notes, look through them and try and be organised for my surgery.'

'Before you go,' Peter said, 'David's going to be off until after New Year. Is there any way we can twist your arm to stay?'

She hesitated, looking from Peter to Oliver and back again. They both looked quite innocent, and Oliver shrugged, as if to imply that it was nothing to do with him.

Did she believe him? Probably not.

'Can I let you know? I'm supposed to be going to Yorkshire. I don't know how long I'll be there.'

'Sure. It doesn't matter anyway, we can't get anyone else, so do what you want—not that there's any pressure,' Peter added with a wry grin.

'Of course not.' She smiled back and, scooping up her notes, went out to her consulting room.

Had he put Peter up to it? Goodness knows. It would seem likely. Damn. She was going to have to tell him, to take the bull by the horns and tough it out.

She'd do it tomorrow night, she decided. Friday. Before she went away for the weekend. Or Saturday, perhaps. But before she went to Yorkshire at least, and then he could think about it over Christmas and they could talk when she got back. It would give him time to consider all the options and work out what he wanted to do.

That decided, she turned her attention to the notes, scanned through them and pressed the button for her first patient.

Nothing was destined to go Kate's way. She psyched herself up to talk to him on Friday night, but he was working for the out-of-hours service from eight until midnight, and as her surgery didn't finish in the end until nearly seven, that didn't leave very long.

She told herself she wasn't really relieved, but she. was. She'd phoned the surgery in Ipswich about the play furniture, and gave Mandy the information on Saturday morning.

'I'd tell Peter but he's in surgery already,' Mandy said. 'He's had three emergencies already this morning, and it's only ten past eight. We don't start for nearly half an hour!'

'Oliver didn't get in until nearly one,' Kate replied. 'I was going to let him sleep in and cover for him, but Peter phoned and said it looked busy and were we both coming in? He'll be down soon.'

'It's because it's Christmas on Monday and this is the last surgery,' Mandy said flatly. 'It's just dawned on them they've got to go to the central emergency surgery from now until Wednesday morning, and all their aches and pains have come out of the closet.

You wait. They'll all be wanting their indigestion remedies ready for Christmas Day.'

Kate chuckled and went through to her room with a cup of coffee. She may as well start as soon as possible, she thought, and by ten-thirty she was glad she had. The seemingly endless stream of patients had finally ground to a halt, and she was about to leave when a young man came in and perched on the chair. He looked edgy and nervous, his leg was jiggling rapidly and she had a bad feeling—nearly as bad as the unwashed smell that was coming off him in waves.

'Oh. I thought I'd finished. I'm afraid I don't have notes for you. I'll ring through,' she said.

'There's no need for that. I don't have notes, I'm a temporary resident. I just need my methodone.'

His eyes were sliding all over the place. 'A temporary resident?' she said, wondering how to get rid of him safely. 'I'm afraid I can't give you methodone, in that case.'

'Yeah, you can. You can give me anything you want,' he said, his voice suddenly menacing. 'Diamorphine, temazepam—all sorts.'

Oh, lord. His hand was sliding towards his pocket, and she was just waiting for him to pull out a knife.

She smiled unconvincingly. 'There may be a way. I need to see if I can get round the computer—'

'No. Just write it out, on a pad.'

'But I don't have one. It's all right, the computer system works,' she said, trying to reassure him. 'I just have to tell it you're someone else.'

She pressed 'Control' and 'P', and then a few other keys, killing time, wondering where on earth Oliver was when she needed him. In fact, it was less than three seconds.

'OK, Jarvis, what the hell are you doing here?'

The man swore, lunging forwards and taking a swing at Oliver, but he was too quick. He grabbed him by the wrist and had him slammed up against the wall before the others had even arrived.

'Oh, not you again. You're banned, Jarvis,' Peter said, sounding bored. 'Mandy, call the cops. Let's get rid of him.'

'They're coming. That's why I was so long. I saw him sneak in. There's a patrol car in the area—and that sounds like them.'

The sirens wailed to a halt, and seconds later Jarvis was outside, being whisked away to discuss his pressurising tactics with the law, and Kate was opening her window and trying to get rid of the smell.

'Your panic button works,' she said with a shaky smile, and Oliver gathered her into his arms and crushed her against his chest.

'The man's a hazard. Are you all right?'

'I'll live,' she said, wondering how close she'd come to that not being true. If she'd been on her own...

His arms tightened, and she hugged him back and then moved out of his arms.

'Well, I suppose I ought to go and get on with my Christmas shopping,' she said with a wry smile. 'I've only got this afternoon. I leave for Yorkshire in the morning.'

'Not unless the forecast has changed since I heard it on the way here,' he said. 'Heavy snow, drifting— Yorkshire's cut off, and the M1 and A1 are closed north of Sheffield. I don't think you're going to get there.'

'Oh, rats. They said it might happen.' She sat down

heavily in her chair. 'I'll go to Norfolk, then,' she said, imagining a Christmas on her own, with no food and the fiftieth rerun of *Mary Poppins* on the telly.

'Stay with me,' he said, making it sound as if it were just any other day. 'I'm going to Steve and Julia. They'd be delighted to have you, too.'

Kate contemplated it, then shook her head. 'No. That isn't fair. They wouldn't want me—'

'They would. They've already asked, and I told them you'd got other plans. They'll be delighted, and one more mouth won't make any difference. Mum and Julia will have over-catered hugely, they always do. I'll tell them you're coming.'

He bent over and pressed a firm, possessive kiss on her lips. 'I need to shut down my computer. Stay here, and don't get into any more trouble. And then we're going Christmas shopping.'

# CHAPTER TEN

IT WAS a beautiful day. Amazingly, there'd been a scattering of snow on Sunday night, not enough to be dangerous but just enough to give the countryside that magical Christmas-card feel.

The roads had been gritted and were clear by the time they'd walked the dogs and set off for Steve's. Oliver had refused to give Kate her present that morning—said he was saving it for later. It was sitting next to his under the little Christmas tree in the corner of his sitting room, and it was just one more thing to dread during the day to come.

Because she was dreading everything, she discovered—his mother, Julia with her kind and gentle but insidious pressure, Steve with his warm acceptance of her, the children. Most especially the children, she thought, and her chest tightened with apprehension.

She was shutting down, she realised, withdrawing, pulling away to a safe place inside herself, but there was nowhere safe. Inside her, with the truth, was the worst place she could imagine.

They arrived to find Steve and the children in the front garden, making a snowman, and their arrival was greeted with shrieks of delight and a clamour of Christmas greetings.

'There isn't enough snow,' Ben complained. 'I want to make a *big* snowman!'

He held his arms outstretched, and Oliver laughed. 'Probably not enough for that!' He shot Kate a glance. 'You OK to go in and make yourself at home while I help this lot?'

He was itching to play with the children, she could see that. 'Just a big kid,' she said with a smile that hopefully wasn't too strained.

She went in through the front door, calling out as she entered, and Julia appeared at the end of the hall with the baby in her arms and greeted her with a hug and a huge smile.

'Happy Christmas!' she said with real feeling, and handed her the baby. 'Here—cuddle your niece. She's being demanding and I want to get on with the lunch.'

'You aren't doing too much, are you?' Kate asked, the doctor in her overriding the pain of holding the baby.

'No, I've got Elizabeth to help,' she said over her shoulder as she went back to the kitchen. 'Oliver and Kate are here,' she announced, and Kate met his mother's eyes and wondered which of them was less enthusiastic about this meeting.

'Hello, dear,' Elizabeth said. 'Happy Christmas.'

'And you. Can I help?'

'Yes, you can hold the baby and tell us what we've forgotten,' Julia said with a laugh. 'Sit down.'

Kate sat on a chair at the groaning table and stared in amazement at the piles of food. 'I shouldn't think you could possibly have forgotten anything,' she said weakly.

'Oh, it's been known,' Elizabeth Crawford said, busying herself at the sink with a pile of vegetables big enough to sink the *Titanic*. 'I think we're all under control today, though.'

Redundant, Kate turned her attention to the baby, and discovered her unblinking stare.

'Hello, my gorgeous,' she said softly. 'Do you have a name yet?'

'Oh, we're still fighting,' Julia said with a laugh, and then her smile slipped. 'Well, not about the name, really. More about whether or not we can use it.'

'What?' Her brow creased into a puzzled frown.

'Katharine,' Julia said simply, and Kate stared down at the baby again, her little features blurring through the tears. 'I love the name,' Julia went on, 'always have, and it goes with the others, and—well, you reappeared at the time, just out of the blue. It seemed appropriate, really. What do you think?'

What could she say? Wait and see if we're still together once I tell him I can't have his babies? He couldn't go through life being reminded of her every time he looked at his little niece.

'It's up to you,' she said, hoping her voice was steady. 'It's your baby, after all.' Her finger was clasped in the baby's tiny fist, and she marvelled at the strength of that small hand.

'I think it's inappropriate,' Elizabeth said, and the atmosphere in the kitchen became suddenly hostile.

'Oh, Elizabeth, not now,' Julia pleaded.

She put her knife down. 'When better? The men aren't here. What are you doing with my son, Kate? Trifling with his emotions again? He's been through hell. Don't do it to him again.'

She closed her eyes against the scalding tears, and Julia tutted and came and put her arm around her.

'Don't pay any attention to her,' she advised softly. 'You must do what you know is right for both of you.'

'But I don't know,' Kate said, the sobs rising. Thrusting the baby at Julia, she ran out of the kitchen and sought sanctuary in the cloakroom. Idiot, she thought. It's Christmas Day. Don't spoil it for them all. But the baby...

'Kate?'

Oliver's voice came to her through the door, and she dragged in a deep breath and swiped away the fresh river of tears. 'Yes?'

'Are you all right, darling? There's a queue.'

Darling. Oh, God. 'I'm fine. I'll be out in a moment.'

'OK.'

She heard the babble of children's voices, and the thunder of their footsteps up the stairs—going up to the bathroom, presumably—and she washed her face and stared at her blotchy and red-rimmed reflection in despair. Oh, for sunglasses, she thought desperately, and carried out some running repairs. She'd still had her bag over her shoulder when she'd fled from the kitchen, and in it was her make-up because she'd anticipated this.

Two minutes later she gave up. It was as good as she could get it, and if she could just avoid everyone's eyes for a few minutes, she'd be fine.

She let herself out, to find Oliver propped up on the wall opposite the door, arms crossed. He shrugged away from the wall, his eyes searching her face. So much for her plans.

'Are you all right?' he said gruffly. 'Julia told me what Mum said. I've already killed her.'

She shook her head in despair. 'Don't kill her. She loves you.'

'Tough. It's none of her business. Go and see her. She's crying in the kitchen.'

He laid a gentle hand on her shoulder, and propelled her towards the kitchen door.

'Kate, I'm so sorry,' Elizabeth said, looking up from the table. Her face was streaked with tears and she looked old and exhausted.

'Don't be. You just love him. Well, so do I.'

'You might tell me that.'

She turned into Oliver's arms and hugged him. 'You know I do.'

His arms circled her again and he held her close against his heart. 'Right,' he said after a moment, his arms slackening. 'Let's get on with Christmas. We've got a heap of presents in the car, and if we don't start soon, we'll still be eating that lot next Christmas.'

She laughed softly and eased away from him, smiling gratefully up at him. But his answering smile was as strained as hers, and his eyes were wary.

Oh, my darling, she thought sadly. What will become of us?

Then the kids poured into the kitchen, chattering and laughing and clamouring at their uncle for presents, and Julia was telling them off for being disgusting and the whole party moved through to the sitting room.

It should have been easier then, Kate thought, but the children were all over Oliver, and he was wonderful with them. He'd put her name on their presents, too, and every now and again one of them would come and show her something, but for the most part it was Oliver they wanted.

And he gave himself to them in spades. After lunch, when they could hardly move for food, he sat on the big sofa with children heaped all over him and around him, and she was put into the comfy chair with the baby on her lap out of the way of the chaos while Julia went upstairs for a rest.

Elizabeth was in the kitchen, Steve was clearing the dining room and they were left alone—if one could be alone with five children! Somehow she doubted it.

They watched television for a while, catching the tail end of a film, and every now and again Kate was conscious of Oliver's eyes on her, checking that she was all right. If he only knew, she thought. Then the children dragged Oliver onto the floor to play with their toys—except that he was the best toy of all, of course, rolling round with them on the floor and allowing them to use him as a horse.

He crawled round the floor on his hands and knees with up to three children at a time teetering on his back, shrieking and giggling and kicking him like jockeys, and he played along like a star. His face was alive with love and laughter, and she felt torn apart.

This is what he should be having, she thought, a huge, busy family, with all the love and chaos and responsibility that it entails. He was made for it, in the way that only some people were, and she couldn't think of a crueller trick of fate.

The baby squirmed in her arms, her rosebud lips pursed and sucking, and her little fists started to flail. After a moment her face puckered up and she started to cry, just little hungry whimpers at first that quickly turned into a full-blown wail.

Steve appeared in the doorway with a rueful smile and scooped up his tiny daughter in big, gentle hands, and with a grin at his younger brother on the floor, he took the baby off to her mother.

Oliver looked at her. 'Are you all right?'

She nodded. 'What about the dogs?' she asked, clutching at straws.

'They'll be all right for a while. I would have brought them, but the house isn't really big enough for four excited children, two dogs and all that food.'

Kate winced at the thought, and he grinned. 'We'll have a cup of tea in a minute. They must be just about finished in the kitchen, and Julia will be down soon.'

She came down then, in fact. Plonking herself into the corner of the sofa next to Kate, she hitched up her jumper and started to feed the baby. Kate looked away so she didn't have to see those moist, rosy little lips beaded with milk latched onto the swollen, blue-veined breast, but she could hear the suckling noise, ramming home to her the fact that her breasts would never fulfil their function.

'Tea,' Elizabeth said, handing Kate a mug, and her smile was tentative and apologetic.

'Thank you,' she said, touching the older woman's hand in a gesture of conciliation. She squeezed it back briefly, then went back to the kitchen for the next wave of mugs and, unbelievably, more food.

They waded through mince pies and Christmas cake, and then Oliver looked at his watch and disentangled himself from the children.

'Time to go,' he said. Ignoring the children's wails of protest, he pulled Kate to her feet, handed her her coat and ushered her towards the door.

'Thank you so much,' she said to Julia, and her sister-in-law's eyes filled with tears.

'Don't be silly,' she said unsteadily. 'It's been lovely to have you. I'm sorry about earlier, I could have killed her.'

'Don't. Leave her alone. She's right.'

For a second Julia said nothing, then she reached out her arms and hugged Kate tightly. 'Stay,' she whispered. 'Don't go again. You're so good for him.'

Kate just hugged her back wordlessly, and then, after a quick hug and a kiss from Steve and a wave at Elizabeth, they were out of the door and away.

'It's nice and quiet,' Oliver said with a laugh as they drove home, but she'd seen him playing with the children and she knew how much he'd enjoyed it.

The journey was uneventful, and he walked the dogs while she filled up the wood-burner again and got it going properly and put on the kettle.

'Do you want supper?' she asked when he came in, and he just laughed.

'I never want to eat again. I just want to hold you,' he said, his laughter fading. 'I want to take you to bed and make love to you—but first I want you to open your present.'

'I've made tea.'

'Good. We'll take it through.'

He sat down on the floor by the tree, patting the floor beside him, and she knelt down and took the box from his hands and opened it. It was a bracelet—delicate and simple, in white gold with tiny diamonds set at the ends of the narrow bars that made up the links. It was beautiful, and her heart contracted. She didn't deserve it.

'I've had it for five years,' he confessed. 'I'd got it for you for Christmas, but you left at the end of November. I couldn't bring myself to take it back.'

She trailed a finger over the cool, smooth links and blinked away tears. 'It's lovely. Oh, Oliver—'

'Shh.' He drew her into his arms, his mouth finding hers, and the presents and the tea were forgotten. He

took her upstairs and made love to her with aching
tenderness, and then again, much later when the dogs
were settled for the night, and afterwards, as they lay
on their sides facing each other, his fingers traced her
cheek, following the path of the tears that had fallen
so many times that day.

'It was a good day, wasn't it?'

Kate's heart twisted inside her. 'You seemed to be
enjoying yourself with the children,' she said, avoid-
ing the issue and addressing it all at the same time.

'We could have all that, you know,' he murmured.
'The kids, the baby, the whole family thing. That
could be us a few years down the line—a real family.
You could come off the Pill and maybe this time next
year we'd have a baby of our own.'

Words deserted her. What could she say that
wouldn't break his heart and destroy all his dreams?

'Think about it,' he said, his voice persuasive.
'We've always wanted children, and the clock's tick-
ing. We're not getting any younger.'

No, she thought in despair. Her clock had stopped,
like the grandfather clock downstairs which had finally given up the ghost last week and sighed to a
halt. The difference was it was two hundred years old.
She was just thirty-one.

He put a finger on her lips. 'Don't say anything
now. Just think about it. Go to sleep now.'

He folded her into his arms, and she lay there, eyes
wide open, staring into the darkened bedroom. Which
way to turn? What to say? How to tell him?

By the morning, she knew. She kissed him goodbye
when he went off to work, covering the morning shift
at the out-of-hours co-op, and then got out of bed on

legs that didn't quite seem to belong to her. She washed and dressed calmly, packed her clothes and other bits and pieces into the car and walked the dogs over the fields behind the house.

It was crisp and sunny and gorgeous, but her heart was shattering into a million pieces and she was numb inside.

She wrote him a note, and propped it up on the middle of the island unit in the kitchen, with the bracelet in its box lying in front of it, and then, having locked the door, she put her key through the letterbox and got into the car and drove away.

Oliver turned onto the drive and frowned in puzzlement, then shrugged. Perhaps Kate had decided to nip into the sales. They started on Boxing Day, and she'd always loved shopping.

Whistling softly, he let himself in and crossed the kitchen, the white paper of her note catching his eye immediately. Then he saw the box, and his footsteps slowed.

'Oh, God, no. Kate, no, not again.'

His fingers shaking, he picked up the note and unfolded it, scanning it with eyes that suddenly blurred.

'Oliver, I can't do this. I'm sorry. I love you. Kate.'

He crumpled it slowly in his fist, waiting for the pain, feeling nothing at first but disbelief and a deep, debilitating cold that crept through him, leaving him numb.

The pain, he realised, would come later.

'Idiot girl,' he said, his voice cracking. Grabbing the phone, he keyed in her mobile number and listened to an electronic voice telling him it wasn't possible to connect his call.

'Damn.'

He'd phone her mother—not that it would get him anywhere, but he had to do something. The phone rang and rang, and he remembered they were up in Yorkshire with her brother. He had no idea what their address was, and her maiden name wasn't rare enough to make Directory Enquiries an option.

He read the note again, straightening it out on the butcher's block, and as he did so his hand knocked the box with the bracelet in it to the floor. The bracelet spilled out, the diamonds sparkling brilliantly in the sunshine, and he stared at it numbly. Damn her, how could she do this to him?

How could she say she loved him? He knelt down to pick it up, his fingers shaking, and the sparkles spread and blurred. The numbness was going, replaced by a pain far greater than any he could have imagined.

He pressed a hand to his chest, amazed at the pain. Did hearts really break? A sob fought free, then another, and he felt the soft, gentle pressure of Muffin's body against his. He put his arm around the dog, clinging on for dear life, because this time, he knew, she'd gone for ever.


'So, that's it. Your daughter definitely has Prader-Willi syndrome, I'm afraid, but the good news is there's a great deal of help and support out there for you now that wasn't available to you before. Your hospital appointment should come through soon, but in the meantime we'll notify Social Services and they'll be in touch.'

The Baileys nodded. They looked numb. Oliver

could identify with that. Apart from agonising waves of grief, he felt numb all the time.

'I knew,' Eve Bailey said heavily. 'Not what it was, of course, but that there was something. I was hoping to see Dr Kate, to thank her for spotting it and sorting it all out, but I gather she's left.'

He held himself together and nodded. 'Yes. She was only here on a temporary contract.'

'Well—could you pass on our thanks? She was very kind, and we're most grateful.'

'Of course,' he agreed. Did his mouth smile? It was instructed to, but it might not have understood. The Baileys didn't seem to notice. They stood up to leave, and he sat back in his chair with a shaky sigh and rammed his hands through his hair.

How could he pass on a message? Her mother, back now from Yorkshire, was consistently blocking his attempts to contact her, and he'd given up.

It was Friday night, nearly three weeks since Kate had left, and with David better and Anne back in the country, he had the weekend off. He could go home and carry on sorting out the house, he supposed—getting the boxes dealt with and the junk thrown out so he could put the house on the market.

He couldn't stay there—not now, with all those memories.

He walked home in the dark, with just the glow of the streetlights to guide him, and went into the kitchen, patting the dogs absently. He let them out and put the kettle on, and then there was a tap at the door.

'Oliver? Can I come in?'

'Looks like you are,' he said drily, and Judy gave him a crooked smile.

'Sorry. Habit.' She looked down at her hands, suddenly awkward. 'Any news of Kate?'

He turned away, busying himself with mugs. 'No. I don't expect there to be. Tea?'

'Thanks. Look, I know it's none of my business, but you look like hell. You've lost loads of weight, you've got dark circles round your eyes and it's as if you're not there any more.'

That's because I'm dead inside, he could have told her, but he didn't. 'So what are you going to do about it?' he asked lightly. 'Feed me up? I don't want to eat.'

'Go and find her.'

'Where?' he exploded. 'How?' His voice softened. 'I'm sorry, but there isn't any way. I don't know where to start looking, and I can't possibly comb every road in Norfolk for her car!' He sighed and rammed his hands through his hair. 'Not that I haven't thought about it.'

'What about contacting the health authority? Pretend it's to do with work?'

'Tried that. She got there first. They won't give out her address or phone number to anyone that doesn't have it.'

'Her mother, then.'

He laughed, and even to his ears it was a bitter and cynical sound. 'She won't even let me over the threshold.'

'Have you tried?'

He hadn't, of course. He'd phoned, constantly, but he hadn't gone there. He shook his head.

'Go. No one could look at you, Oliver, and not take pity on you. It's not as if you're a monster. You haven't hurt her.'

'I don't know what I've done to her,' he said, his voice cracking, and he turned away again, dragging in a steadying breath.

'It can't hurt to try. I'll have the dogs for you. I'll take them now. You go. I'll see you whenever.'

And without waiting for an answer, she picked up the beanbags, the bowls and the food, and headed for the door. 'I'll be back in a minute.'

By the time she came back he'd turned down the heating, locked the house and was waiting at the gate with the dogs. 'I don't think it'll make any difference, but you're right. I have to try, one last time.'

He leant over and kissed her cheek, and she hugged him briefly and took the leads. 'Go on. And drive carefully. And ring me.'

It took him two hours to get to Peterborough in the Friday night traffic, and he arrived at her parents' house just as they finished their evening meal.

'Oliver.' Her father's eyes scanned him rapidly and he shook his head. 'Good God, man, you look awful. Come in. Alexandra?'

She came, and when she saw him her eyes filled with tears. 'Oh, Oliver, I'm so sorry.'

'Where is she?' he asked, and, despite telling himself he wouldn't allow it to happen, he felt the tears well in his eyes. 'I need her, Alex. I can't live without her...'

He broke off, dragging in air, his jaws clamped together to keep in the pain, and she tutted and shook her head.

'Oh, Oliver, she begged me not to tell you. She made me promise, but I can't see you like this, either of you. It just isn't fair. You have to go to her—and make her tell you the truth this time. Don't take no for an answer—promise me.'

'I won't,' he said, then hesitated, preparing himself for the pain. 'Alex—she's not dying, is she?'

'No. No, she's not dying, but she might as well be, the way she looks. Just go to her. Hugh, have you written it all down?'

Her father handed him a piece of paper with her address and telephone number on it. 'She'll be there. She doesn't go out much, and it'll be after ten by the time you get there.'

Oliver nodded, took the paper and studied it.

'Here.' Her father showed him the location on a map, and pushed it into his hands. 'Go.'

He went.


Kate lifted her head and listened, and heard it again— the faint ringing of the doorbell downstairs. Then a banging on the door, and a voice calling her name.

Oliver.

Panic clawed at her, but there was no escape, and then suddenly she was calm. It was time.

She got out of bed, pulled on her clothes and walked slowly downstairs, flicking on lights as she went. She turned on the porch light and opened the door, just as his hand was raised to thunder on it again, and it fell slowly to his side.

He looked awful. Dreadful—and it was going to get worse.

'Come in,' she said, stepping back to allow him into the room. He ducked his head under the low doorway and followed her through to the kitchen, his footfalls loud on the tiled floor.

'Tea or coffee?' she said, and he stared at her.

'For God's sake, Kate, what the hell is this all about?' he asked, his voice raw with pain.

Her hand hovered for a moment, then she turned away from the kettle and lowered herself to a chair. 'Sit down.'

'Will I need to?'

'You look as if you're about to fall, so probably.'

He sat. Opposite her, his elbows on the table, his eyes locked on her face. 'Tell me,' he said. 'Now. Please.'

She nodded. 'OK.' She opened her mouth, but nothing came out. Funny, she'd rehearsed this so many times, but the words just weren't there any more, and she didn't know how to start.

Oliver was losing patience. If she strung this out any longer, he was going to die of heart failure. 'Kate, just spit it out,' he growled.

She shrugged. 'I've got premature ovarian failure,' she said finally, her voice colourless. 'My system just shut down—five, six years ago. I'd been told a week before I left you. That's why I went—because I knew how much you wanted a family, and I couldn't give you one. I still can't. I won't ever be able to.'

He stared at her blankly, the reality of her words slowly sinking in. 'And so you left me? Just like that? Without discussing it?'

He felt anger rising to the surface of his boiling emotions, and he slammed his hand down on the table and stood up, knocking the chair flying. 'You just decided that if we couldn't have children, we didn't have a marriage? Is that it? What is it with you and unilateral decisions?'

He bent over her, his face inches from hers, the

anger boiling over in him. 'This is *our* marriage, Kate, yours and mine. Not just yours. You can't make those sorts of decisions for me.'

'But I didn't,' she said flatly. 'You did.'

'What?'

'You had a patient, in your training practice. She'd been diagnosed with POF. You came back and said she was still single, and old before her time. ''Poor woman,'' you said. ''Who's going to want her?'' She was younger than me.'

He felt the blood drain from his face. 'Kate, I felt *sorry* for her.'

'I know. And I didn't want your pity.'

Oliver shook his head, stunned. 'You could have had my grief—and my love. Did they matter so little to you? Dammit, do *I* matter so little to you that you could just walk away?'

'I couldn't bear it…if you pitied me. And you would. Poor Kate—she isn't even a real woman.'

'Oh, for God's sake, don't try that one. Of course you're a real woman.'

'I don't feel like one.'

'Depends on your perspective,' he said with a last vestige of humour. 'Any more woman and my heart would pack up.'

'Don't give me platitudes,' she said flatly. 'It's true. I'm not. I'm just an empty shell—old, worn out— I've got nothing to offer you.'

Oliver stared at her, horrified. She believed it. She actually believed that rubbish. She was holding herself rigid, he realised, her hands clenched together so tightly they were bloodless. He took them in his. 'Katie, don't do this to us,' he said raggedly. 'I love you. I'll always love you. I can't live without you.'

'But you want children. You could have them with someone else—'.

'I don't want someone else's children,' he yelled, straightening up and slamming the chair back onto its feet. 'I want your children—our children.' His voice fell away to almost nothing. 'If I can't have them, I'll be sad, of course, but not like this. Not torn apart, unable to function, dead inside. I need you, Kate. I'm nothing without you.'

'You'll get over me—in the end. You could marry Judy—'

'Would you stop it?' he ground out. 'I don't want to marry Judy! I'm married to you—I love you. I don't want anyone else, and I won't. Not ever. I want you. That's why I asked you to stay on—not just for Christmas, but for always. When I came home—when I found your note...'

His voice broke, and she shook her head, grief and despair written all over her face. She didn't believe him, wouldn't be convinced, and what more could he say?

Oliver closed his eyes, unable to bear the ravaged look on her face any longer, and then he felt her arms creep round him.

'Oliver?'

'Oh, Katie...'

His arms wrapped round her, crushing her against his chest, and he ruthlessly fought down the sob that rose in his throat. He had to be strong—had to talk her round, convince her...

'I wish I could believe you,' she whispered brokenly. 'I've spent five years convincing myself that I was doing the right thing, longing to be with you, missing you so much...'

His chest heaved, and he crushed her harder against him. 'Idiot,' he said unsteadily. 'Why wouldn't you talk to me?'

'Because I know you. I thought you'd insist on staying with me, doing the decent thing, and I had visions of us years down the line with you hating me, feeling trapped out of an over-developed sense of duty.'

'Duty?' He laughed shortly, and held her away, staring down at her with tears welling in his eyes. 'Does this look like duty? Kate, I need you.'

'Oh, Oliver, I need you, too, so desperately, but I thought if I let you go...'

His arms tightened round her again, hanging on like grim death. 'Don't think. Just promise me that. Don't ever, ever think for me again. Five years, Kate. Five years we've been apart, both of us sad and lonely and desperate. How could you do that to us?'

Her shoulders shook. 'I'm sorry. Oliver, I'm so sorry.'

His body curled around, sheltering her, his heart melting. 'Ah, love, don't cry. Not any more. Just come home with me—let's start again.'

'Tomorrow,' she promised. 'Not now. Not tonight. Tonight I just want you to hold me, and maybe tomorrow I'll let you go for long enough to drive home.'

He lifted his head, staring down into her tear-filled eyes, and dredged up a crooked smile.

'Maybe. Maybe we'll just stay here for ever.'

She laughed, a sad, ragged little sound, and laid her head back against his chest. 'Take me to bed.'

'My pleasure,' he said, and, scooping her up in his arms, he carried her up the narrow little staircase to the bedroom.

'Oliver?'

'Mmm.'

Kate smiled indulgently. He was tired. Of course he was—he'd spent all night proving to her that she was a woman, and at last, finally, she was able to believe him.

She stood up from the window-seat, with one last glance out at the gloriously sunny, frosty day, and went over to the bed, sitting down and pulling the quilt away from his face.

'Hey, lazybones.'

'Mmm.'

'It's a lovely day.'

Oliver opened his eyes and looked at her, and smiled tenderly, his hand coming up to cup her cheek. 'Of course it is. You're here—and we're together again, finally—and for good, this time, I hope?'

She smiled, dispelling the sudden doubt in his eyes. 'Count on it. You won't get rid of me again.'

'Good. Come back to bed.'

'No. I don't want to wear you out, you've got to last me the rest of my life. Anyway, we have to get up. We've got people to tell—your family, mine—'

'Judy. She's dog-sitting for me. You'll have to thank her, she sent me.'

Kate felt her heart expand to take in the world. 'I'll do that,' she said with a smile, 'just as soon as we get home.'

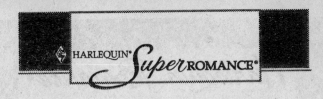
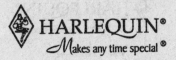

# HARLEQUIN®
# INTRIGUE

## WE'LL LEAVE YOU BREATHLESS!

If you've been looking for thrilling tales of
contemporary passion and sensuous love stories
with taut, edge-of-the-seat suspense—then
you'll love Harlequin Intrigue!

Every month, you'll meet four new heroes
who are guaranteed to make your spine tingle
and your pulse pound. With them you'll enter
into the exciting world of Harlequin Intrigue—
where your life is on the line
and so is your heart!

## THAT'S INTRIGUE—
## ROMANTIC SUSPENSE
## AT ITS BEST!

HARLEQUIN®

*Makes any time special* ®

# Harlequin® Historical

*From rugged lawmen and valiant knights to defiant heiresses and spirited frontierswomen, Harlequin Historicals will capture your imagination with their dramatic scope, passion and adventure.*

*Harlequin Historicals . . . they're too good to miss!*

HHDIR1